10/96

LIVING WITH GHOSTS

ALSO BY PRINCE MICHAEL OF GREECE

LIVING WITH GHOSTS

Eleven Extraordinary Tales

Prince Michael of Greece

Translated by Anthony Roberts
Photographs by Justin Creedy Smith

W. W. Norton & Company

New York • London

For information about permission to reproduce selections from this book, write to Permissions,
W. W. Norton & Company, Inc., 500 Fifth Avenue, New York, NY 10110.

The text of this book is composed in Garamond No.3
with the display set in Nicholas Cochin Bold.
Composition by Crane Typesetting Service Inc.
Manufacturing by The Courier Companies Inc.
Book design by JAM.

Library of Congress Cataloging-in-Publication Data

Michel, Prince of Greece, 1939-
[Ces femmes de l'au-delà. English]
Living with ghosts : eleven extraordinary tales / Prince Michael of Greece;
translated by Anthony Roberts; photographs by Justin Creedy Smith.
p. cm.
Translation of: Ces femmes de l'au-delà.
ISBN 0-393-03952-8
1. Ghosts. 2. Haunted castles.
GR580.M53 1996
398.2'094'05—-dc20

W. W. Norton & Company, Inc., 500 Fifth Avenue, New York, N.Y. 10110 http://web.wwnorton.com

W. W. Norton & Company Ltd., 10 Coptic Street, London WCIA IPU
1 2 3 4 5 6 7 8 9 0

To M.J.
To my parents.

CONTENTS

"I had no sooner passed through the paper-thin barrier which divides life from death, than I knew absolute joy and peace were at hand. Then I was dragged back. The light was near and I could not come at it. But in that moment I gained the certainty that one day I would be admitted. My banishment is only temporary. . . ."

The Lady of Grazzano

PREFACE

"ONCE UPON A TIME IN ATHENS THERE WAS a house which was large and commodious, but cursed by ill-fame. In the dead of the night, there would be a sound of clanking metal; followed by the clatter of chains, first in the distance, then at closer quarters; after which appeared the spectre of a gaunt, ragged old man, with a long beard and shaggy hair. The spectre's feet were fettered and with his hands he shook the manacles that bound his wrists.

"The people who lived in the house spent their nights stark awake with terror, and many grew ill and died. Even in the full light of day, when the spectre was nowhere to be seen, their eyes were filled with its presence, for fear will always feed on itself.

"The house was at length left empty, completely abandoned to its ghost. Nevertheless the owners put up a sign offering it for rent or sale, in the event that some buyer or tenant, ignorant of the circumstances, should come forward.

"Now it happened that the philosopher Athenodorus came to the city; he saw the sign outside the house, and the very low price of it aroused his interest. He made enquiries, found out the facts, and in spite of (or perhaps because of) the ghost, resolved to rent the house for his own use.

"At nightfall, he had a bed set up for himself near the entrance, and called for tablets, a stylus and lamps, after which he sent all his servants to their sleeping-places at the back of the building, whilst he himself settled down to work. Athenodorus concentrated all his mental attention on his studies, as well as the sight of his eyes and the skill of his hands; this he did deliberately, in order that his imagination should not be left free to suggest supernatural sounds and thus assail him with groundless fear.

"To begin with, there was silence in the house. Then Athenodorus heard in the distance the sound of ringing metal and the clank of chains. He did not raise his eyes, nor did he put down his stylus, but continued obstinately attending to his work, which he set up as a barrier against what he heard. But the sound grew louder and ever closer, until at last it reached the threshold of the room and entered in. At that instant Athenodorus turned; he recognized the figure behind him as the one he had heard described. The apparition beckoned with its finger, but the philosopher made a sign that it should wait awhile, and turned his attention back to his tablets. The figure, not to be denied, approached and stood over him as he wrote, beckoning and rattling its chains most mournfully. Whereupon Athenodorus took up his lamp and prepared to follow where it led.

"The spectre moved slowly, as if crushed by the weight of its chains. It led Athenodorus into the courtyard of the house, where it abruptly vanished. Not a whit taken aback, the philosopher made a little mound of grass and leaves to mark the exact spot: and the next day he fetched the magistrates and told them to dig exactly there.

"The magistrates did as Athenodorus directed, and unearthed a tangle of chains and human bones, stripped clean of flesh by the action of time and damp. The magistrates ordered these bones to be gathered up and fitly buried elsewhere.

"After this, the house of Athenodorus was no longer haunted, the shade of the dead man having been provided with a proper resting-place."

This story dates from the first century after Christ, and its author was Pliny the Younger in his *Letters*. It is a proof, if any were needed, that ghosts have been part of human existence for time out of mind.

Caesar appeared to his assassin Brutus, probably to sharpen his remorse. In the reign of Louis XIV, the prettier maids of honor attending the Sun King's mother, Anne of Austria, often fainted with terror while crossing the long gallery at Fontainebleau, because François Premier, the oversexed French monarch who died two centuries earlier, would frequently appear to them "robed in a green dressing gown patterned with flowers."

On May 5, 1821, Madame Mère, otherwise known as the mother of Napoleon Bonaparte, was living in retirement in a gloomy palace in Rome. A man came to the door who refused to reveal his identity beyond the statement that he had come "from St. Helena." Alone with this man, the old lady saw him draw back the mantle covering his face and was amazed to see the face of her son, the emperor. Believing that Napoleon had somehow escaped his jailers, she was ready to fall into his arms: but the figure drew back slowly into the antechamber, where it passed out of sight. Madame Mère followed; not only did she find the room empty, but her footmen assured her that they had seen nobody go by. Several weeks later she learned that on the day of this mysterious visit the emperor had breathed his last, on the tiny British island of St. Helena far away in the Atlantic.

Shortly after the drowned body of Ludwig II of Bavaria was discovered, his ghost paid a visit to the king's cousin and confidante, Empress Elizabeth of Austria, and talked to her "about the other world." King George V of England, who even as a cadet in the Royal Navy was completely destitute of imagination, observed a phantom galleon passing a few cable lengths from his ship, while on watch alone on the bridge.

After the death of her only son, the Prince Imperial, in a skirmish with Zulus in South Africa, the Empress Eugénie insisted on visiting the scene of the tragedy. After a long voyage from Europe, she was at last shown a broad, empty plain: but nobody knew the exact spot where the prince had fallen. The empress paced to and fro across the ground; finally she halted and declared that her son had died where she was now standing. How did she know? She replied that she had caught a strong odor of violets at that exact point. The prince had always worn a particular cologne made with the essence of violets.

In effect, ghosts manifest themselves not only to our senses of sight, hearing, and touch, but also to our sense of smell.

Some ghosts also have the gift of ubiquity. Famous figures such as Anne Boleyn and Mary, Queen of Scots, combined beauty, passionate love affairs, and tragic ends; they now appear, with or without their heads, in different places that featured in their breathlessly exciting lives.

Henry VIII, having executed Anne Boleyn, had her buried in an unseemly hurry—which, as later events were to show, was far from satisfactory to her shade. Not long ago an officer assigned to the late night watch at the Tower of London noticed that the stained-glass windows in the Chapel of St. Peter were illuminated from within. Investigating, he found the door firmly locked, so he brought a ladder and clambered up to one of the windows.

What he saw within nearly knocked him off his perch.

Along the aisle of the chapel moved a cortége of lords and ladies in the dress of the early Tudors, all in deep mourning.

Bringing up the rear was a lady in especially sumptuous robes: for a while the officer could only see her back, but when the figure reached the altar she turned full face. From the portraits he had seen, the officer recognized Anne Boleyn. The beheaded mother of Queen Elizabeth the First was directing her own phantom burial—only this time the thing was being done amid all the pomp a queen has a right to expect.

A tragic end does not necessarily spawn a ghost. To my knowledge Marie-Antoinette, the most tragic of queens, has only been seen once, in the 1930s. The witnesses were a couple of venerable English ladies who relived (in complete ignorance of the facts) the dramatic events that occurred at the Trianon on October 5, 1789.

As to the murdered Czar Nicolas II of Russia, he is content to show himself from time to time on a servant's staircase in the Winter Palace. He usually appears to sentinels who do not recognize him, but who are nonetheless very terrified and invariably request to be transferred, choosing the most distant garrison duty in preference to the horrid sinecure of patrolling the czar's former residence.

Finally, ghosthood is not necessarily confined to the great and famous, appearing to special initiates in great houses and palaces twitching with history. Who cannot remember, at some moment in their lives, the slight creak of a door on a windless night, or footsteps echoing from an upper floor of an empty house? And who has not—at least once—sensed an unseen presence in a building they have never visited before? If we were all prepared to acknowledge the existence of the inexplicable, many more of us would include ghosts among our acquaintances.

In my view, everybody is perfectly capable of communicating with ghosts, or rather with the unusual dead. It is one of the human faculties we all of us possess from birth, and which we subsequently allow to atrophy. The vast majority of people only develop a fraction of the powers they were born with, in this department.

All the same, some people are constitutionally more receptive to phantoms than others. Once, while visiting the royal shooting estate at Sandringham, my father was taking a pre-prandial rest, lounging on his bed with a book of memoirs. Suddenly he found his gaze drawn toward the window, through which he saw the outline of a woman dressed in a very antiquated and particular style. A curious mask covered the woman's face; nonetheless my father intercepted a pathetic glance that seemed to implore his aid.

It happened that my father's valet was with him in the room, busy with his clothes, and my father, who knew very well that he was in the presence of a ghost, asked the man out of interest if he could see anything unusual. The valet stared at him, uncomprehending. Later, at dinner, my father related what had earlier befallen, to the great amusement of his nieces, who taxed him with engulfing more whiskey than was wise.

A few days later, the house party was taken to visit another giant country house nearby. My father saw his nieces go up to the second floor. Moments later they came flying down, twittering and calling his name. He was led into a long gallery crammed with portraits, in the midst of which he instantly recognized a painting of his ghost, exactly as he had described her at the dinner table: only this time she held the mask in her hand, and the face was bare. The caretaker explained that she was an ancestor of the present owner of the house; she had been incarcerated by her husband, who was mad with jealousy of her great beauty. The unfortunate prisoner sought to throw herself on the mercy of the king: in vain, for she died a prisoner. Since then (added the caretaker), she was supposed to appear periodically to the descendants of the kings of England, still forlornly seeking their aid.

I myself can say that I was raised on the most familiar terms with ghosts, given that my mother's family was just as gifted as my father's as far as the supernatural was concerned. For example, before I reached the age of sixteen I had the signal honor of hearing the *"tête qui crie"* at the Chateau d'Eu. This macabre object, a human head carefully processed by the head-shrinking Jivaro tribe of Brazil, had ears that were perfectly miniaturized: and given that the ears are the hardest part of the head to get right, even for a master shrinker, the *"tête qui crie"* was something of a rarity.

The head was kept in a glass case in a curiosity room on the ground floor, and it had an unpleasant habit of groaning miserably each night. My cousins and I heard it regularly and as clear as a bell from the upper floor, where the salons were. We would run like hares down to the haunted room, but as soon as we burst through the door the groaning ceased, much to our annoyance.

So ghosts run in my family's veins, so to speak, and from my earliest youth I have been used to accepting both their existence and the part they play in our own. When I meet up with my cousins in a house none of us has been to before, the first thing we do is chivy out its dead occupants like so many ferrets. We delve in our own sensibilities, exchange impressions, and generally massage the various essences till we see them emerge from invisibility and take shape before our eyes. No doubt other people think we're crazy, but all the same we are sufficiently convincing to create, even in the most skeptical minds, a quiver of ingenuous doubt.

Fairly rapidly, I learned in the ghost field to do without the stimulation of an entourage of others who felt (or thought they felt) the same way as I did. Visiting places for the first time, I found that, even without consciously wishing to, I had clearer and clearer impressions of the supernatural, to the point where I at last felt myself capable of meeting irony and incredulity head-on.

When my wife, Marina, and I were first married, in the 1960s, we were guests on the ground floor of an eighteenth-century mansion on the Quai Malaquais, beside the Seine in Paris. We occupied a large bedroom with a columned alcove, in which I liked to sit and work or read. On several occasions, when Marina was out, I found myself glancing up from the page having sensed some kind of presence which seemed to have entered noiselessly. This happened at all times of day—morning, afternoon, and evening—and eventually the phenomenon became so frequent that I had to acknowledge that there was a ghost in the room with me. True to form, I wanted to know more about him (or her) and while I busied myself with my various occupations, I took care to sharpen my antennae.

The ghost seemed to possess a distinctly feminine quality; but above all it exuded—or rather embalmed—a powerful eroticism. This impression grew and grew. Finally, one evening at dinner with friends in the dining room next door, I openly declared that our room was haunted by some kind of erotic

ghost. This announcement was greeted with lewd hoots of laughter. I let it pass: we eventually moved away from the Quai Malaquais, and I forgot about my ghost. But a few months later, our former host received a letter from an organization calling itself the Société des Amis de Franz Liszt, telling him that his home had once served as the composer's bachelor apartment, and that at one time the columned bedroom had been the scene of Liszt's passionate cavortings with Marie d'Agult.

I kept on having experiences like this, until I was compelled to admit that I possessed a special sensitivity in the matter of ghosts. I decided to cultivate this gift (for I took it to be a gift) as much as I could, and at least to get the measure of it, if not find some kind of explanation for what I constantly observed. I immersed myself in books about ghosts, scrupulously avoiding literary work and concentrating on sober scientific records.

I also made my own researches, traveling around and visiting places which were said to be supernaturally inhabited. And these travels finally brought me to Leap, said to be the most haunted castle in Ireland. The house certainly looked the part; it stood in a bare country of peat bog, its charred, ivy-covered ruins rearing into the perpetual mist. Burned out and desolate, it seemed to me a miracle that Leap was standing at all.

The sheer numbers of its ghosts had given

it a truly fearsome reputation. From a wall on the first floor had emerged a creature so terrifying that the lady who witnessed it never recovered from the shock. But this was a mere *avant-goût*: the attic chapel, for example, had been the setting for much more impressive apparitions. In front of the altar, a priest had been hacked to bloody shreds in the very act of performing Mass; and a pair of hate-crazed duelists had leapt to their deaths from one of the highest Gothic window embrasures.

Nevertheless, when I arrived at Leap I was immediately drawn to the cellars. Such impulses I have learned to obey: without attempting to understand why, I made my way down a dark, narrow, slippery staircase, which led to a vault dimly lit by a small basement window.

Here I sat down on the dank floor and composed myself to receive whatever might come to me. No corrupted corpses sprouted from the walls: but I knew before a very few minutes had passed that there was something far worse in this place.

A prodigious destructive power was horribly couched beneath my feet. I could feel the hum of it. I knew this power had lain buried here from time immemorial; no doubt it manifested itself indirectly from time to time, by the medium of violent episodes and tragedies. Now dormant, it was no less awesome, but in its essence it had strictly nothing whatever to do with ghosts.

Thus the traces of blood which appear in some houses, the objects that shift suddenly without the agency of a human hand, are in my opinion the result not of dead souls manifesting themselves, but of energies which normally remain dormant, but which can be activated by certain empowered human presences. Countless strange, inexplicable phenomena are caused by forces unrelated to hauntings.

In the cellar at Leap, with a foul dragon dozing under the soles of my feet, I felt fear; but still I knew myself to be in no danger. We all have powers protecting us, upon which we can call, and I am no exception.

After this disagreeable experience, I decided to cross the Rubicon and write openly about ghosts. A magazine commissioned articles from me on the subject. I selected a number of houses that were known to be uncommonly "charged" and went to visit them.

My researches eventually led me to Schloss P., a former commandery of the Teutonic knights and a Baroque garrison building of a kind peculiar to Germany. The reason why this house must remain unnamed will emerge from the account that follows.

It was a rainy afternoon. I had been earnestly promised a "Red Lady" and a "White Knight." These phantoms had been seen by a number of reliable witnesses, some of whom had heard them as well. One man had let off both barrels of a shotgun at a fleeting figure, while another had actually succeeded in obtaining that rare article, a color photograph of the ghost—in this case, the Red Lady.

We were received by an aged and infinitely fatigued baroness, who had clearly once been handsome, but who had been in some sort *déclassé* by a chronic and continuous shortage of money. Indeed she had been driven to the necessity of doing a great deal of hard work around the house. There was also a son-in-law, a handsome, rather arrogant son of the people who appeared inordinately proud to be the new lord of the manor, and had evidently succeeded in silencing, if not thoroughly terrorizing, his wife's mother. This pair kindly showed us round the castle, pausing gravely on the stairs and in the corridors and bedrooms wherein the most violent apparitions had occurred.

I took notes avidly, delighting in the certainty that here at least I was on to something exceptional. As soon as their evidence had been recorded, my photographer, Patrick, settled down to work: but since Patrick works with that unbelievably maddening attention to detail which all talented photographers seem to share, I decided that I would tax my hosts' patience no further.

I asked their permission to wander through the house alone, which they very graciously granted.

So I set off in the direction of the second floor, where I gravitated to a broad vestibule, soberly furnished, but bathed in the sunshine which by now had broken through the clouds. Being somewhat weary, I sat down on a straight-backed chair facing a quite extraordinarily hideous full-length portrait of an eighteenth-century empress.

Vague thoughts and images began to drift through my mind: and little by little calm descended on me, until I became aware that another presence had slipped into the room. At this point I am not sure if my eyes were open or closed: in any case, I knew for sure that this was neither the medieval knight nor the Renaissance lady I had been told about. It was a woman, right enough: but a woman of my own time and century. Moreover, she was *confined to a wheelchair*.

Immediately I sensed furious rancor. I took care to remain as passive as possible, only listening. I heard nothing, no doubt because all these impressions were coming from within me. Instead I perceived what seemed to be a series of ideograms which then changed into silent words. They were not the words of some unknown voice speaking inside my mind, but the workings of a mind foreign to me which, so to speak, took the place of my own mind and then formed words and phrases. My brain no longer operated under the direction of my will, but under the direction of someone else's will, or frequency; that somebody else having commenced to use it as a conduit.

The first coherent signal was a torrent of abuse against the old baroness I had left downstairs. During her lifetime, it seemed, the paralyzed creature in the wheelchair had fed and sheltered the baroness, cushioning her with affection: for which the baroness had repaid her by stealing her husband, and getting pregnant with his daughter. But (said the wheelchair) the baroness would never keep possession of the castle, for soon enough everything she had so treacherously acquired would vanish like the dew. Her handsome son-in-law would spend every penny she had, and the property would have to be sold.

I don't know how long this vindictive tirade lasted, but no detail, no reproach, and no accusation were spared me. Finally the words ceased to come, and I found myself alone again, somewhat perplexed in my mind. I turned to face the setting sun, whose orange rays blazed against the Cordoba leather that covered the walls. I was sure I hadn't invented what I had just heard; still, I was suspicious of my own imagination. There is, after all, a very thin dividing line between imagination and the perception of a very distant, sometimes inexplicable truth: one which is at all times difficult to comprehend, and virtually impossible to verify. Nevertheless my curiosity had been aroused—and, as I discovered shortly afterwards, so had that of my hosts. I had been absent for about an hour. The baroness and her son-in-law plied me with questions. Had I seen the "white knight"? I must at least

have seen the "red lady." I muttered that I had neither seen nor felt the least thing, and fled as soon as I decently could.

On the way home, I interrogated the friend who had brought me to Schloss P. And this is what he told me: just after the Second World War, the owner of the castle had married a princess of high lineage, who went down with polio a few years later and was confined for the rest of her life to a wheelchair. Her husband found the perfect person to look after her and keep her company, an impoverished baroness. What should never have been allowed to occur, of course occurred; the husband and the companion conceived such a passion for each other that they cast aside all restraint, even in the presence of the wretched paralytic. A daughter was born, who grew up and married the tyrannical blond individual who was now cock of the roost.

This involuntary experience raised a number of burning questions, to which I knew there could be no answers. All I could do was give up any attempt at analysis and continue to cultivate the faculty I possessed.

There are ghosts of all ages and social classes, and they can be found anywhere and everywhere you go: on a road, in a hotel, in a theater, in a cinema, on a train, on a plane, or in an ultramodern office block.

In this book I have chosen female ghosts as my theme, purely because women have been the subject of the biographies which have hitherto brought me so much good fortune. I embarked on it out of curiosity, to find out more about the true nature of ghosts, and the reasons which reduce some of us to the ghost state when we die. I had no doubt that if they wished to do so, the ghosts themselves could teach me this. And what is more, these wretched beings, whom we should all pity rather than fear, perhaps stand in great need of us, the living.

Lastly, I set out to write this book with a particular ghost story at the back of my mind. This is my favorite in the genre, because I believe that its *d'enouement* may well be applicable to every one of us.

In the 1960s, an Englishwoman, eminently down-to-earth, wealthy, happy, and ordinary, dreamed each night of her life the self-same dream. In it she saw a house, a large and distinctive country mansion in an unmistakable landscape. She recognized neither the landscape nor the building, and she often wondered why both returned to her so regularly as she slept.

One day, while traveling through Scotland on a second honeymoon with her husband, she drove around a corner and saw plainly before her the house she had dreamed of for so long. Resolving to solve the enigma once and for all, she stopped and rang at the door.

A surly-looking man, whom she took to be the caretaker, answered the bell—and stood there staring at her with open horror.

She asked who lived in the house: shaking, the caretaker replied that it had been empty for many years, the owners not caring to share it with the White Lady.

"So the house is haunted?"

"You should know. You are the ghost."

LIVING WITH GHOSTS

CASSANDRA

La Rocca di Soragna, Province of Parma, Italy

THAT EVENING, GIAN FRANCO, the Prince of Soragna's trusty maitre d'hôtel, retired early to his bedroom on the second floor of the castle of La Rocca di Soragna. There was little work for him to do, because the prince and his family were away at their château in Burgundy, inherited from some French ancestor. But Gian Franco didn't have the heart to go out and enjoy his leisure, for he knew that far away in France the prince was very ill indeed.

It was August 1983, and the night was stifling hot. Sleep eluded Gian Franco. Soft sounds wafted through his open window from the romantic park around the house. Suddenly he sat up in bed: somewhere in the house, doors and windows were beginning to flap. He tried to work out where the noise was coming from and concluded it must be the stucco drawing room, the one "she" liked best. Before long, doors and windows were banging in unison in the first-floor galleries, the frescoed loggias of the second floor, the throne room, and the great princely apartment with its enormous heavily gilded armchairs. Gian Franco, quaking with fright, found himself unable to move. The din became deafening: it was as if the heaviest pieces of furniture, the marquetry commodes, the ornamental cabinets, were being pushed and shoved and slammed against the walls of the great house from basement to attic.

Then, as suddenly as it had begun, the din ceased.

The night was as silent as before. Gian Franco rose, dressed hastily, and hurried down the stairs. In the ground-floor servant's hall he found the rest of the staff routed from their beds, like him frightened and shaken. Gian Franco gravely uncorked a bottle of grappa and poured everyone present a stiff drink. They all knew exactly what the phenomenon meant, and now they sat in silence with their glasses, waiting. Five minutes later, what they knew would happen, happened. The telephone rang, and a faraway voice informed Gian Franco that the Prince of Soragna had just breathed his last, across the Alps in Burgundy.

Twenty years earlier, in 1963, Gian Franco had witnessed an exactly similar incident in the family. One of the prince's uncles had fallen ill at a neighboring house, and the family was preparing to pay him a visit. Just as they were climbing into the car under the courtyard arches, the doors and windows of the ground-floor salons suddenly banged open and shut, raising an unholy racket.

"At this point, there's no more need for us to go," said the prince sadly, and indeed a few minutes later the news came through that his uncle was dead.

For centuries, every death in the Soragna family has been heralded in this way, and with particular violence when the person concerned was the head of the family. And on every occasion those left alive have murmured the same word: "Cassandra."

In June 1991, I happened to be at Soragna filming a television documentary. The camera crew and I had crossed the heavily populated, board-flat, oven-baked plains south of Milan. The village of Soragna seemed to us more like a small township, and our first move on our arrival was to plunge into the joyous bustle of a weekly market.

A short distance away lowered the silent silhouette of La Rocca, a giant cube of brick, unadorned and mortifyingly severe.

But as I soon discovered, La Rocca's treasures, like those of the great palaces of the Orient, lay concealed out of sight. Inside, the spacious rooms frothed with Baroque stucco and the long galleries abounded in idyllic landscapes. I walked through frescoed loggias and gilded, sumptuously furnished ceremonial apartments, saw portraits of resplendent ancestors, and passed vaulted salons decorated in the purest Mannerist style of the Renaissance. Above all there was the supreme luxury of sweet, cool air, in which the succession of rooms, corridors, and deserted staircases were exquisitely steeped.

The stories told to me by friends who had stayed at the castle, as well as articles in the sensational Italian press, had brought to my attention the existence of Cassandra di Soragna, an ancestor of the present owners.

I succeeded in tracking down Gian Franco in his gloomy lair and set about extorting the details of what had happened to him. The other members of the staff treated me with a certain reserve; the gardener, for one, wouldn't go so far as categorically to deny the existence of the ghost of Cassandra, but he had gardener's doubts about her. The estate carpenter proclaimed himself a strong but puzzled skeptic. The village priest was circumspect, after the manner of his kind, though he allowed that odd things had happened up at the castle . . . Anyway, after an afternoon of relentless prodding it eventually became quite clear to me that the inhabitants of Soragna unanimously believed in the ghost, and were scared out of their wits by it.

This Cassandra, I thought, must nurse an insatiable craving for vengeance, to appear so noisily at the approach of a corporeal detachment within the princely family.

Only the incumbent prince's mother, Violetta di Soragna, remained completely unimpressed by all the fuss. She was the last on my list of interviews. I could see that she had once been a fascinating beauty, and even now, though well over eighty, her character remained unconquerable. I found her in the garden, where, benchbound on account of a multiple fracture, she was sniping at pigeons with her rifle.

Principesa Violetta knew all about Cassandra, naturally. Was she afraid? She'd never been afraid in her life, of anything or anybody. But this was such an *aggressive* phantom, I insisted. The princess's deep blue eyes twinkled ironically, and I noticed the dark rings beneath them.

"I have a gentleman's agreement with Cassandra," she said. "She doesn't bother me, I don't bother her. We get along swimmingly, she and I."

And there matters rested for a while.

Three years later, in December, I returned to Soragna. The heat had been replaced by penetrating cold. Inside the castle the chill was worse than in the open air. The dowager Princess Violetta had died, and my appointment now was with her son.

When Justin and I arrived at the gate, it was four o'clock and the light was fading fast. I shuddered as I walked across the courtyard, now innocent of the orange trees and palms that I remembered from my last visit. A servant showed us into the prince's office: it was a high-ceilinged, vaulted room, dimly lit. Maps, framed diplomas, and one or two photographs decorated the walls. The prince received us with a warmth that belied his austere surroundings, and he lit a cigarette as we settled into a pair of well-used armchairs.

Diofebo Meli Lupi, Prince of Soragna, comes from a long line of Italian princelings. His family, which has been famous since the high Middle Ages, at one point succeeded in building up its own independent state in Italy. The Soragnas struck their own coinage and administered their own justice, and their castle of La Rocca still boasts an authentic red-and-gold throne room. In the basement there is a vaulted dungeon which was routinely used as a torture chamber, with chains dangling from the ceiling and, in one corner, a frescoed niche that served as an oratory for the poor wretches facing execution. Today this dungeon is a cellar stuffed with good wine.

The convulsions of the Renaissance enabled the shrewd lords of Soragna to entrench themselves in their region, but in the following centuries the new order imposed by the great powers—along with Italy's growing decadence—trimmed away their power and independence even as they amassed fresh titles and honors.

The present head of the family is a thoroughly contemporary individual. Courteous, hospitable, and good-natured, he is an ardent motorcycle buff, an impenitent pursuer of fur and feather, and a tireless traveler. He has never been afraid in the great castle, where he lives entirely alone. Yet he not only believes in the ghost of Cassandra, he has a radically different point of view about her.

About twenty years ago, while he was doing his military service, Diofebo was out on maneuvers with some fellow cadets when a force he compares to a "muscular hand" grasped his shoulder and forced him to bend forward. At that instant, a salvo of machine-gun fire loosed by an inexperienced soldier passed so close overhead he felt the wind of it. The "muscular hand" had saved him from certain death.

Later, he was riding his motorcycle very fast along one of the dead-straight roads around Soragna when for some reason the machine abruptly slowed. He applied the accelerator without effect; something was holding the bike firmly in check. At that moment a tractor chugged out a hidden gate and entirely blocked the road: by all rights, Diofebo should have hit it fair and square. He was entirely convinced that in this case, too, Cassandra's hand had intervened to save his life.

Late one evening in October 1992, the

prince was sitting in his armchair, reading, when he noticed that the adjustable arm of his standard lamp was shifting perceptibly to the right. He realigned it, whereupon it again began to swing sideways. This occurred several more times before Diofebo, by now convinced that Cassandra was beside him, said to her mentally: "If you have something you mean to tell me, make the lamp describe a complete circle."

The lamp immediately did so.

Next morning, the dowager princess, who had been hale and hearty all her life, suddenly felt poorly. It was the beginning of her final illness. The months succeeded one another and her state worsened. Then, in January 1993, while he was at her bedside, Diofebo saw the two doors of the huge old wardrobe slowly swing open. Perhaps someone had left them ajar; he got up, closed them, and locked them securely. Lock or no lock, the same thing happened again—and again a third time. The key had no effect whatever. Diofebo glanced at his watch, which stood at exactly 5 p.m. Three days later, his mother died at exactly that hour. He was convinced that Cassandra had come to give him warning, so mother and son could prepare themselves for the final parting.

Since that time, Diofebo's links with his ancestor Cassandra have grown closer and closer, and the relationship is now so warm that one wonders if today this curious ghost isn't just about his favorite companion.

"I know she's just as attached to this house as I am myself. Cassandra is a friend, almost a sister to me." Thus, at La Rocca di Soragna, where the atmosphere seems unchanged by the passage of time, the *bon vivant* latest scion of the family cohabits affectionately, even lovingly, with his invisible yet entirely present ancestor.

Who is Cassandra? A frightful messenger of death, or a ghost hopelessly besotted with her own descendant? I went to consult the prince's secretary, archivist, and family historian. This person's realm was the enormous castle library, several rooms packed from floor to ceiling with venerable books, parchment volumes, and family papers, and he told me what I wanted to know. . . .

Cassandra Marinoni lived in the sixteenth century. She belonged to a family of minor but absurdly wealthy aristocrats, and therefore she married the present prince's namesake, Diofebo di Soragna, who at that time was a marquis with the rank and privileges of a sovereign.

Cassandra had one sister, Lucrezia, to whom she was very close. Lucrezia married Count Giuliano di Anguissola, a gambler, adventurer, and Lothario, who married her for her mountains of gold ecus. But as it turned out Lucrezia was deaf to his demands for money, which led in short order to furious scenes and eventually a complete separation. Anguissola went his own way and Lucrezia remained in her palace at Cremona, often visiting her beloved sister at Soragna. "And so their lives went on, until that fatal afternoon of June 18, 1573," concluded the librarian.

He led me to Cassandra's portrait, where it hung in the billiard room with the rest of them. The figure was superb and haughty: the rigid carriage and angular features seemed more apt to inspire respect than affection. The eyes were glittering and disdainful, and the lips seemed ready to utter some shattering oath. The fingers toyed menacingly with a small dagger. Perhaps I was influenced by Gian Franco, but benevolent or otherwise I knew I was looking at a woman with a very powerful personality.

I took my leave of the librarian and wandered into the next room, called the Hercules Room, which was largely unaltered since Cassandra's time. The legs, arms, and wings of stucco angels poked out of the walls. Colored frescoes soared into the high vaulted ceiling, illustrating the various exploits of Hercules. Apart from a few chairs, the room was empty, but through the broad windows poured the pale light of winter, setting the polished floor aglimmer.

Everyone had agreed that Cassandra was rowdiest in this room; so, fighting hard against a cold so biting that my clothes were no protection against it at all, I sat down in a high-backed sixteenth-century chair and closed my eyes.

I immediately saw the red-and-gold lower half of a long dress, a few feet away in the middle of the room. The details emerged in succession: the bodice with its gold embroidery, the short velvet train, the wide, flared sleeves. A woman's silhouette was now crystal clear before me; only her face remained ill-defined.

In my lifetime, I never thought myself especially interesting. I was rich, of course, but money was taken for granted in the world I moved in, and I paid it little mind. I left my fortune in the hands of experts, who looked after it efficiently and not too dishonestly. I was intelligent and cultivated, like most ladies of my time; I was also a strong character, with a taste for authority and an uneven humor which made people call me difficult. I knew nothing of passion, and I did nothing with the culture I had acquired, using it neither to appreciate beautiful things nor to collect them. I kept up my religious observances, though I spurned all fanaticism and had no deep yearning for Christ. I had much more appetite for earthly sustenance, and I suppose if I had one weakness it was my love of food and drink. In every other

wise, everywhere and always, I was measured to the point of dullness. My true image in no way resembles the portrait in the room next door, which shows an impressive personality. That portrait was painted after my death and is no likeness at all. I wasn't beautiful and I knew it and I hated the fact. And that's why I show you my figure, not my face.

So it wasn't on account of my beauty that the Marquis of Soragna married me, but on account of my money. It didn't take much brains to see that. My husband was incapable of hiding what he felt, and he made no attempt to conceal his satisfaction at having netted an heiress. At the same time, a kind of mutual respect and esteem existed between us. I was no hand at politics, but I was able to give him sound advice. Though Soragna was sole master in his own fief, he was nonetheless a pocket sovereign, a prey to powerful neighbors like the Gonzagas of Mantua, the Farneses of Parma, and other such sharks. He was constantly under pressure to take sides with one or the other, constantly intriguing to preserve his independence, and above all trying to back the one which would emerge as the winner. Here I was able to help him, and on the whole we respected one another.

I was quite sure he was unfaithful to me but I didn't care to think about it. I imagine he had brief affairs with women of low condition, village strumpets and farm girls from round about. For my own part, men didn't interest me any more

than I interested them. Naturally I was fond of my children and they returned my affection, but in general my maternal feelings weren't especially strong.

Nor was I particularly attached to La Rocca di Soragna, which was my husband's stronghold, though I maintained it in the proper style. I never traveled far afield, either, preferring to pay regular visits to our various properties nearby. In general my indifference to the world was active rather than passive; as far as I was concerned the obligations imposed on me by my condition lent sufficient interest to my life.

And then there was my sister. If anyone could lure me from my lassitude, Lucrezia could. She wasn't as bright as I was, but she was much prettier, and like me had a husband who had married her for her money, that worthless swindler Anguissola: though I have to admit he disguised his motive more adroitly than Soragna, being a smooth talker who knew all the tricks.

Anguissola was handsome and attractive. He could be infinitely charming—and infinitely odious, if you dared to cross him. He was a lavish spender, too, though the money never went on women. He may have had numerous mistresses, but he used their cash rather than vice versa. Nor did he gamble. No: his constant need of lucre sprang from the disastrous fact that he fancied himself as a shrewd man of business. He was forever involving himself in doomed ventures. In Italy, you have to remember, we nobles were openly interested in money and in the ways it could be obtained. My own father, who was a minor aristocrat, dedicated his entire life to amassing gold; and the children of wealthy merchants were forever marrying into noble families.

Well, Anguissola loved to take risks in business. Lucrezia saw her fortune begin to dwindle, and she promptly refused to advance her husband any further funds. Whereupon he turned cold and threatening, and more than once he badly scared me. As for Lucrezia, she was too angry and high-spirited to be scared. Little by little, she grew to loathe her husband so cordially that their formal separation, when it came, was a mighty relief.

Then Anguissola changed his tack completely and sought a reconciliation. Lucrezia believed he had changed for the better. "You see," she crowed, "I was right to hold him in check! He's coming to heel!"

I wasn't so sure. Anguissola's sudden change of heart appeared to me deeply alarming. "Be careful," I warned Lucrezia. "He's a double dealer. God knows what he may be planning."

"You're wrong. I know him inside out. I just needed to cut off the money."

"Be careful, all the same."

Naturally Lucrezia asked me to be present at their reconciliation. I agreed to join her in Cremona, knowing she needed me. She was reassured by Anguissola's request to see her, but she was apprehensive about meeting him face-to-face.

So Anguissola had suggested that I come too, as an arbiter.

To my relief I arrived at Lucrezia's house before he did. Nobody knew exactly when he would appear.

It was after lunch, a hot summer's afternoon. Lucrezia and I were together in an inner room she had fitted out especially for such weather. We had changed into light shifts to rest.

Dozing, I felt a curious sensation stealing over me. The silence seemed unnatural. It was the hour of siesta; everyone was resting, even the servants, on account of the heat; but there was no sound of cicadas, nor humming insects, nor birdsong, and this was very eerie. Even when a house is quiet, it breathes. In that moment I realized I had ceased to hear the breathing of the house. I said so to Lucrezia, but she rolled over to face the wall.

"Leave me in peace, let me sleep . . . "

Then I heard them. At first a rustling, followed by stealthy footfalls: several people were making their way up the stairs outside. The chambermaids? No—these steps were too heavy and hesitant. They halted at the door while I lay paralyzed with terror.

Lucrezia, as usual, was quite without fear. She too had heard the footsteps and she was merely curious to know who our visitors could be at this hour.

Then the door burst inwards. They grabbed us, yelling and roaring, and some pinioned our arms *while others stabbed and hacked at us with blades, again and again.*

My blood was everywhere. I heard Lucrezia shriek. It happened suddenly, within the space of a minute: but that minute seemed endless, as memories, feelings, and sensations blurred my mind. Men were letting out my life with dagger thrusts but I felt no pain. It was as if I had fallen into two halves, as if the assassins were knifing someone else. Long after it was no longer necessary they continued to gouge at our inert bodies, out of pure delight. They were professional killers, but greater than their desire for gain was their lust for blood.

Then there was nothing, neither the cries of Lucrezia, nor the sated grunts of our murderers. I heard no sound, I only saw the red blades rise and fall, rise and fall. I was outside my body. I was already dead.

A trap had been laid for us. Anguissola needed gold, and since Lucrezia stubbornly refused to give him any, his option was to kill her and assume her fortune. He had been preparing for this moment over a long period. It was child's play to hire a gang of professional killers, but to secure the complicity—or at least the neutrality—of the authorities required time and judicious bribery. Anguissola had bought allies, but above all he had rendered the lords of Cremona certain services which made him untouchable, involving matters so shameful and scandalous that his silence was paramount. In short, he had done enough to ensure

that the sovereign would wink at whatever he did to his wife.

The only other person in a position to cause him any trouble was me. Anguissola knew this all too well, just as he knew that I did not trust him. Had I remained alive, I would have denounced his involvement in Lucrezia's murder. I would have made quite sure that he was arrested, tried, and executed. So he had to kill me too. As for my husband, Anguissola knew he would never join the plot: had he mentioned the idea directly, Soragna would probably have betrayed him. But Anguissola also knew that his brother-in-law loved money as dearly as he did, and in the event of my death Soragna stood to inherit my fortune, just as he himself stood to inherit Lucrezia's.

So Anguissola gambled that Soragna's avarice would keep him silent, and in a roundabout fashion he made sure that a vague rumor of what was about to happen reached the prince's ears. Soragna was well aware that his brother-in-law was in financial difficulty, and he suspected that Anguissola might make an attempt on Lucrezia's life, and probably on mine too. Anguissola's suggested reconciliation, and his invitation to me to come to Cremona and take part in it, cannot have left him in any doubt. Soragna knew what was afoot and did nothing to avert it.

My brother-in-law was a devil, but my husband was worse.

Afterwards Soragna arranged for me to be

buried with the utmost pomp, publicly demonstrating both the depth of his grief and the magnificence of his estate. My catafalque was nearly as tall as the church itself, and a forest of candles burned on its steps. He caused crowns to be festooned upon the structure in token of my rank; and to the accompaniment of celestial music, a concourse of bishops in golden vestments officiated over my corpse, amid dense clouds of incense. My husband did not go so far as to shed a tear, but throughout the ceremony he looked as stricken as was commensurate with his dignity. It was revolting.

Anguissola was immediately indicated as a silent accomplice in the murders, but Anguissola had vanished. The magistrates issued warrants for his arrest and alerted the authorities in neighboring states: but the man couldn't be found, or rather nobody bothered to look for him in the place where he could be found. After a few years, he reappeared in public and encountered no difficulties. In the interval he had contrived to take control of Lucrezia's fortune.

The Marquis of Soragna's first reaction to the murder of his wife and sister-in-law was an indignant and strongly worded demand for justice to be done. The sovereign of Cremona, the authorities, and the magistrates were all fully aware that he wouldn't insist. He declared at the top of his voice that his fixed purpose was to pursue and punish the murderer of his beloved wife, and everyone who heard him felt reassured that

Soragna, at least, was an honest man. But the tactic was not so much intended to salve his conscience as to supply him with every possible guarantee of future well-being.

Just before, during, and after my moment of death, I experienced a sensation of falling into a bottomless well, of being sucked irresistibly downwards into the darkness. And then I stopped falling. I was surrounded by light and I was within that light. There was my cadaver, riddled with stab wounds and covered with blood, and from it issued my soul, which blended with the light. I cannot say more: except that a part of myself remained behind, the part you call ghost, because at the moment of my passing I had experienced horror, violence, agony, rage, and loathing.

But violent death alone is not sufficient to spawn a ghost. Many have come to death, even violent death, in a different manner, and thereafter their souls have slipped into the light. Others whose deaths held no hint of tragedy, but who did not approach death as they should have done, remain behind as I do. So it is the way in which we effect the passage—passage is a better word than death—which determines whether or not we go directly to the light.

I determined to be avenged—but not on Anguissola. That brute had organized our killing, but he himself met a miserable end, having run through the fortune his crime had won for him. No: my purest hatred was reserved for my husband. His hypocrisy and his affectation of

ignorance were unpardonable. I did not choose to haunt the palace at Cremona where I was betrayed, but La Rocca di Soragna and whoever lived there. I commenced to make my presence felt immediately. I terrorized the courtesans, the servants, the staff, and even the children. Everyone lived in dread, except my husband. In vain did I manifest myself in the most spectacular possible ways—he couldn't care less, and eventually I gave up trying. Soragna died peacefully in his bed, loaded with honors and titles, enormously wealthy, surrounded by his loving family.

It was quite extraordinarily vexing.

I began to wreak what vengeance I could on Soragna's descendants, who proved more receptive than he. For generation after generation, I struck terror into the hearts of the Soragnas. Then, very gradually, a change came about. I began to like them. During my lifetime I hadn't much cared for La Rocca di Soragna. But by dint of haunting the old place, I developed something akin to affection for it. Of course I make a deafening din whenever some member of the family is about to die, but my reasons are benign: I want them to prepare them-selves properly for the passage, and not be caught unawares and widdershins as I was. Of course I frighten people, but in my way I also contribute to the renown of La Rocca. I attract visitors who pay. I'm useful.

As to Diofebo—I mean the Diofebo of today—it is true that I have intervened in his life several times, and he knows that. My craving for vengeance is long gone, and my descendant is perfectly correct in thinking that I like him and wish him well—and try to protect him.

There are many like me. I am alone, and we are many millions, all alone. I cannot describe this state because living people do not have the perceptions, the knowledge, or the openness to understand. For the time being, I am waiting. This waiting is no punishment: punishment has nothing to do with my state, which is the state of invisible reality. Having approached the passage in the wrong way, some element is still lacking which, if it came, would admit me fully to the light. I must acquire that element, during this period of waiting. How shall I, when shall I move into the light?

THE LOVES OF LADY C.

Doneraile Court, County Clare, Ireland

ONE AUGUST NIGHT IN 1887, a farmer was driving to Sycamore from the market town of Mallow. The hour was late, but he trusted his old mare enough to drop the reins and doze as she drew him steadily homeward. Before long the little trap was bowling along in the moonlight beside the park walls of Doneraile.

Branches bent above the lane, thickening the darkness. The farmer, who had often passed this way late at night, was in no way apprehensive: indeed, he was half asleep when suddenly there was a crash of foliage nearby. A large animal burst from the under-growth, bounded across the road ahead, and vanished. By the light of the moon it showed as a tawny, dog-like creature. The farmer, himself in a state of terror, was amazed to note that his mare was quite unmoved, since she continued to trot peacefully along.

Round the next turn they approached what was known as the Canal Gate. In that instant the farmer saw a black coach swerve out of the gateway: and to his horror the four horses galloping ahead of it were all of them headless. The coach wheeled full tilt down the road to Doneraile and disappeared from sight.

The old mare now stopped dead, and

when he recovered his wits the farmer gave her a trembling touch of the whip to urge her forward. But not a step would she go. In vain did he climb down from his seat and try to lead her by the bridle; the creature wouldn't budge from where she stood, quivering and frothing as though she had run a race. And in the end the poor man had to leave her there and go the last miles home on foot, in a state of dread at least as abject as his horse's.

Next morning he heard that the fourth Viscount Doneraile had died in the night, down at the big house.

Ireland, of course, is the motherland of ghosts. It's not that phantoms are more numerous in Ireland than their counterparts elsewhere, only that the Irish themselves agree that phantoms are part of life—to such a degree that they are the natural national topic of conversation, like football or politics among those of other nations. The activities of ghosts are matters of close interest, and their authors come in every shape and form.

Nor are ghosts the only denizens of the other world acknowledged by the Irish. Irish fields and riverbanks harbor such famous magical beings as the leprechaun, whose appetite for ruthless practical jokes knows no limit. The very trees seethe with supernatural creatures, as do certain Irish plants, which human beings trample at their peril.

And all this host of creatures, on account of their number and variety, sow bewilderment in the minds of men. Thus my friend John Nicolas Colclough, a perfect representative of the fantasy, humor, culture, and hospitality of his country, has had the wonderful idea of compiling an inventory of Irish ghosts, which he carries with him everywhere he goes. Thanks to Colclough, ghost-hunting in Ireland is now as exact a business as an African safari.

When I came to John Nicolas, I wasn't in the most optimistic of moods. In fact, I was fed up with the procession of White, Blue, Green, Red, and Black Ladies, one-legged, one-armed, and one-eyed, that everybody was clamoring to show me. John Nicolas therefore suggested I go to Doneraile Court, where, he said, there were so many boarders from the other world that I could take my choice of which to interview. So it came about that one soft January morning I found myself driving with John Nicolas along the narrow roads of County Cork, through that pleasant land of sleepy villages and lively townships. The past, in the form of ruined abbeys, old humpbacked bridges, and towers beetling out of copses, was omnipresent around us. The plump gnarled trees, some standing alone, others consorting in groups, all seemed to belong to some greater enchanted forest.

At Doneraile, we swept past a graceful gateway, drove on through rolling parkland, and finally crunched to a halt before the big house itself, an exquisite manor with the elegant rounded outline and tall bay windows of the eighteenth century. Inside, the building was flooded with sunlight, which entered from every point of the compass.

Arthur Montgomery received us in his library/sitting room on the second floor, which was in fact the only room in the house kept properly heated at all times. He was, he explained, not the owner but the curator: the last of the Donerailes had died in 1967, and after that the place had been abandoned for a decade. It was teetering on the brink of utter ruin when the Georgian Society stepped in to save it. This deed was done at the instigation of Desmond Guiness, then the society's president, who was famous for expending all his energy on preserving just such fine old houses.

As a child, Arthur Montgomery had often visited Doneraile, on account of his family being neighbors and related to the owners. He had loved the place ever since; and now destiny had brought him not only to inhabit the place, but also to give it life, a task he undertook with devotion and enthusiasm.

Arthur's delight in sharing his passion for Doneraile soon made us forget the cold. We wandered through rooms and halls whose decor was gradually reemerging from the years of vandalism. Newly painted in fresh colors, they were empty yet of furniture and fittings, and our footfalls echoed on the bare floorboards.

To visit a great Irish house is to hear, before long, the chronicle of its hauntings.

The Saint Legers, the builders of Doneraile, were a Norman family who came to England with the army of William the Conqueror, leaving behind them in France a senior branch which still prospers. Later, encouraged to do so by the royal Tudors, whose nefarious aim it was to colonize Ireland by stealth, the Saint Legers crossed the Irish Sea to seek their fortune: and in Ireland they found it, amid a cascade of titles, honors, and high offices. But Ireland's spell eventually fell upon them and transformed their line of earthy Norman barons into a succession of eccentric, tragic, and often frightening figures.

Arthur Montgomery showed us a corner room on the ground floor, somberly and elegantly paneled. In the eighteenth century, this served as the office of the Saint Leger who became the first Viscount Doneraile. One afternoon, Doneraile's daughter came here for a quiet hour's reading. She snuggled up by the window, hidden from all comers by the thick curtains, and immersed herself in her book. After a while she heard voices.

Her father had entered the room with some other men, and they were arguing vigorously. After a while the girl realized they were holding a secret meeting of their Masonic lodge. She dared not move a muscle. After a while the meeting broke up, and the girl breathed again: but her relief was short-lived, because the curtains were abruptly drawn back by her father's valet, who had come to tidy the room. The two stared at each other aghast—then the valet, whose loyalty to his lodge outweighed his affection for his master's daughter, ran to denounce the eavesdropper.

The girl was immediately locked in a room while the members of the lodge hastily reassembled to consider what should be done. The only punishment possible for outsiders who stumbled on Masonic secrets was instant death. The horrified father tried to make his fellow Masons relent, but they wouldn't be moved; innocent or not, the girl must be stabbed, beheaded, hanged, or shot.

Then a happy idea came to Doneraile. The only way, apart from summary execution, to ensure his daughter's silence was to make her take the oath and become a full-fledged Mason. The drawback was that no woman had yet been admitted to the order. Fortunately Lord Doneraile's fellow Masons were none of them monsters, and they inclined to this bold solution. The terrified girl was summoned from the cabinet in which she had been held, and enjoined to swear the Mason's oath of secrecy till death. In view of the dreadful alternative, she did so gladly, thus becoming the first female Freemason in Irish history.

The second Viscount Doneraile was a brusque, tyrannical man obsessed with hunting. One day he pursued a stag straight into a farmhouse and demanded that the farmer drive it out to his hounds: but the farmer, standing on his rights, manfully refused to do so. At this, Lord Doneraile was seized by a hideous paroxysm of rage, in which he unleashed a torrent of oaths so terrible and blasphemous that he was condemned in the eyes of the peasantry to pursue his stag for all eternity.

Not so long ago, on a night of full moon, one of the gamekeepers was doing the rounds with his son. All of a sudden they heard the cry of hounds in the park, where all hunting was forbidden. For a moment it crossed the keeper's mind that the Doneraile pack, whose kennels were a mile away beside the canal, might have got loose in the darkness; but then he recalled that the park gates were firmly locked and there was no other way the hounds could have entered. The chorus grew louder and clearer with every

passing moment, till out of the shadows poured a pack of hounds, with a wraithlike rider in a broad-brimmed hat galloping hell for leather after. It seemed to both witnesses that although they could hear the cry of the hounds, they were making no true sound whatever, any more than the hooves of the horse thundering on the earth, as pack and huntsman swept round a bend in the avenue and vanished in the moonlight.

Next morning, no trace could be found in the park of horse or hounds. The mystery of their coming remained total, though it was commonly agreed thereafter that the second viscount had perhaps not entirely taken his leave of Doneraile.

The fifth viscount was also accused of haunting his former seat, on account of the particularly revolting manner of his death. Arthur Montgomery suggested that I pay a visit to the room in which this dramatic incident had occurred. We pulled on our overcoats (in Ireland you dress up warm to go inside, and shed clothes like autumn leaves when you go out) and plodded up the magnificent Adam staircase to the still unrestored third floor.

Here the floors were rickety, the doors creaked, and raw brick stared through the half-stripped paneling. We had to walk along narrow planks to reach the haunted room, where Montgomery related his story.

At the end of the nineteenth century, the then Viscount Doneraile went walking in his park and, together with his *valet de chambre*, was bitten by a fox. The village doctor advised both men to take ship immediately to Paris, in order to consult Pasteur. His lordship accordingly dispatched the valet to France, but considering himself above medicine and doctors, resolutely remained at home. This was an error, because although the valet lived to be almost a hundred, Lord Doneraile very soon contracted rabies. He had to be locked up on the top floor of the house, well out of sight, where before long his paroxysms became so violent that he had to be chained to the bed. Thus the poor man died, foaming at the mouth, shrieking in agony, and straining piteously against the iron manacles that ate into his flesh.

I gazed around me. The captive's bedroom was lit by three tall windows looking out across the countryside, and despite the steady rain falling outside the atmosphere seemed to fizz with gaiety. There was nothing macabre here at all—on the contrary.

Arthur Montgomery shared my opinion, and moreover he was entirely convinced there was no ghost at all in this part of the building. "When I took the house in hand," he said, "I found chains in this room— wagon chains they were, which somebody had dropped here. Someone coming later must have seen them, and made the connection with Lord Doneraile's death. Hence the legend."

The fifth Lord Doneraile had only one child, a daughter. This was the beautiful Claire Saint Leger, who married Lord Casteltown and brought him Doneraile Court as part of her dowry.

Lord Casteltown was a great Irish magnate, whose singular destiny it was to be not only the chief of an Irish clan—the Fitzpatricks—but also an English peer. In addition to this he was (rather oddly) an accredited Druid. Soaring through Eton, Oxford, and the Life Guards, he followed the perfect establishment trajectory of his time; and as a frequent visitor to London he became a close friend of the Prince of Wales, later Edward VII, for whom he arranged shooting parties—shooting was a passion the two men shared—and the occasional romantic encounter.

So well did Casteltown manage these delights for his grateful sovereign that the latter bestowed on him the Order of St. Patrick. But after Edward came the dismal War of Independence which racked Ireland in the 1920s. One day, an IRA group turned up at Casteltown's house at Granston to "requisition" his shotguns. His lordship received the terrorists graciously, spoke to them in Gaelic (which left them bemused),

and showed them round the house. Finally, he invited them into his library for a glass of brandy and a hand at bridge. The terrorists declined, on the grounds that "their masks might appall the ladies."

After this close shave Lord Casteltown saw that his guns wouldn't be safe from the IRA for many weeks longer, and his guns were as dear to him as anything he owned. So in the knowledge that his head gardener was one of the fiercest partisans in the local branch of the IRA, he seized the initiative and presented the man with all his firearms, lock, stock, and barrel. The agreement they hammered out was that the gardener and his boys would use the pieces to shoot policemen and English soldiers on weekdays, and Lord Casteltown would have them on Saturdays for the duck flighting. This worked out very satisfactorily for both parties.

Now Lord Casteltown loved his wife passionately. Claire Saint Leger was fifteen years younger than he, but nevertheless she predeceased her husband, leaving him inconsolable. Every day Lord Casteltown left a packet of sweets on her grave, which were just as regularly purloined by the village boys, thus comforting the brokenhearted old man in the fancy that his dead wife had accepted them. Carried away by this idea, he caused to be built over the grave a small canopy, to keep his darling dry, and this may still be seen today. Moreover, he fell into the habit of slipping love notes into the books in his library, in the hope that Claire—or rather Claire's ghost—would read them.

In the fullness of time Lord Casteltown died of his grief, and it is scarcely surprising that he has haunted Doneraile Court ever since. Many visitors to the house have seen and identified his wraith in afteryears.

When Arthur Montgomery grew up and returned to Doneraile as its warden, he found the house in a dreadful state. Undaunted, he began by moving into a couple of rooms on the second floor and set about the gigantic task of bringing the building back from ruin. One night he heard heavy footsteps pacing to and fro in the dining room below, and being the stout descendant of a long and fearless line, he rushed downstairs forthwith to see what was the matter. The room was empty, of course, and Arthur wasn't surprised. He had absorbed lurid ghost stories about Doneraile Court with his mother's milk.

However, the same phenomenon began to occur every night, and the sleepless Arthur started to give serious thought to the identity of the ghost, and the reason for its comings and goings.

Who better to ask than his good friend Geraldine Saint Leger? This last descendant of the family was a woman of innate class,

the casual paradigm of Irish grandeur. Although the Court no longer belonged to her family, she still nursed an atavistic love of the place, and continued to visit regularly. Geraldine told Arthur Montgomery that her uncle Lord Casteltown, when he was a widower, liked to spend long hours sitting in the dining room alone, lost in reveries of his dead wife. Today, since practically the entire house was devoid of furniture, her advice was to "leave an armchair by the fireplace, and that will settle the man." Arthur Montgomery immediately did as directed, and from that day to this he has never again been discommoded by Lord Casteltown walking the dining-room floor.

On one occasion, however, the ghosts of Doneraile contrived to spring a surprise on their last descendant, who believed until that moment that she knew everything there was to know about them.

Geraldine was pottering round the house, as was her custom, and she came to the bedroom of her aunt, the late Lady Casteltown. There were a few pieces of furniture left there, notably a big four-poster bed. There was also a venerable wardrobe, in which hung a long, dusty dress of beautiful gray silk with black trimmings. It appeared to have been cut for a tall and unusually slender woman.

Nearby was a mahogany dressing table

with an oval looking glass. Instinctively, Geraldine bent over to adjust her hair, and at that moment saw that the mirror seemed obscured by a subtle haze, *not on the outside, but on the inside of the glass.* Gradually, as she watched, this haze dissipated, as if swept aside by an invisible hand. But now, instead of her own features appearing, Geraldine saw the evanescent face of Lady Casteltown. The vision lasted long enough for her to recognize her aunt's wide-set, glittering eyes, full lips, glorious complexion, blond chignon, and regal bearing. Astonished (though not at all frightened) Geraldine closed her eyes. When she opened them again, the relection in the mirror was her own.

Hearing of this interesting adventure, I myself became more and more intrigued by Claire Saint Leger. In all the contemporary documents and descriptions, she seemed to have lived entirely in her husband's shadow. Yet she was also a famous and majestic beauty, a flamboyant personality, and a redoubtable character, if her portrait in the hall at Doneraile was anything to go by. Apart from this, there was precious little information to e found about her, just as if a deliberate effort ad been made in her lifetime to cover her racks. There were only vague rumors.

What did Claire do while her husband was away hunting in Canada for months on end, leaving her alone at Granston or Doneraile? Recently, a store of letters written to her by Judge Oliver Wendell Holmes, the best-known American jurist of his generation, had come to light. Claire was forty-three and Holmes fifty-five when they met; the judge, a notorious ladies' man, immediately discovered a tenderness for Lady Casteltown. How far had this "tenderness" gone, and, above all, how had "Hibernia," as Holmes called Claire, reacted to his passion? Her letters to him were never found, so one can only guess.

Even as a ghost, Claire remained elusive. Her husband was seen and recognized by everyone; but she had appeared only once, to her niece Geraldine, and that in the most oblique way. "Towards the end of her life," said Arthur Montgomery, "she became highly eccentric. She left this magnificent bedroom and moved to a small room on the top floor, where she lived as a recluse until her death."

So once again we climbed the elegant staircase, only this time our destination was a broad corner room with a low ceiling. The few rickety chairs, the eviscerated sofa, and the worn-out wooden chest told of long neglect, though the five tall windows let in a flood of light.

Beyond the windows lay miles of sunlit, undulating parkland. I looked out and wondered: as far as I could see there was no plausible reason, in terms of the social norms of the epoch, why the mistress of Doneraile Court should forsake the lower floor and move to this part of the house, which was naturally reserved for staff. Claire's father, of course, may have done the same, when he died here supposedly in chains, but even if his story were true it was a case of force majeure. Nobody knew, however, what secret motive might have led Lady Casteltown to spend her last days in a servant's bedroom.

The others now left me alone in the room. I continued to contemplate the bare old twisted trees, the river in spate, and the deer grazing peacefully in the distance. The wind rattled the slates above my head and the sun cast pale patterns of the window frames across the worm-eaten floorboards. Month after month, year after year, Lady Casteltown had lived in this room, to which her whole world had been reduced. So thoroughly had she saturated its closed atmosphere with her thoughts, her feelings, and her mysterious presence that she seemed to stand alive and physically present before me. Tall and majestic, she came forward very slowly and halted by the fireplace. Her face was obscured by a vaporous haze, or perhaps by veils, and try as I might I could not distinguish her features.

I was beautiful. I was judged a beauty, and I devoted my life to this fact, or rather to the fasci-nation it had for others. My appearance was my sole passion, and I took infinite pains over it. I had an insatiable hunger for men's admiration. I had lovers aplenty, but did I love them for themselves? I did not. I was obsessed by my own ability to seduce, to the point that I loved that ability more than my own self, glorying in the devastation it wrought. I was drunk with my power over others.

I took my first lover, a farm boy, when I was sixteen years old. I knew there might be trouble should the man I married discover I was no virgin, but I didn't care a rap: and in the event Casteltown was too much in love with me to say a word about it, or even notice. Later on, he passed over many other escapades in silence. He probably had mistresses of his own—though I never had proof of it—but I knew very well he could truly love no other woman but me.

Casteltown far preferred to be in town, but for my sake he settled in the country, making it possible for me to spend my whole life in the landscape I adored. I had an instinctive closeness to plants, trees, animals, and all the elements. How often did I look out on the fields and woodlands from these very windows! Men compared me to a flower, but I was really a wild animal, like one of the does in the park, reveling in freedom.

From my girlhood, or rather from the time when I began to be loved, this room served me well. It was unoccupied, and so a perfect place to bring my lovers. Although a great house like mine was

constantly filled with servants and such, I knew how to move about undetected. I came to this pleasure chamber whenever I chose. I had no need to skulk up the back stairs: I took the high road and never met a living soul, even when the house was filled with people.

My lovers were all of them remarkable for their beauty, or their wit, or their character, or their spirit of adventure. I cared nothing for their social background, my own sufficed me.

In love I looked for a confrontation of the senses, for a subtle alloy not only of bodies, but of personalities. My relations with my lovers were like the nights of love I gave them, sometimes rampant and destructive, like molten lava, sometimes sluggish and gentle as an estuary.

Oliver Holmes was a late arrival. He was more taken with me than I with him, for I preferred men younger; but I admired his intellect and his wide knowledge. His attentions flattered me, and it probably gratified him to pay court to a titled woman. We got along famously, though our relationship was only occasionally physical. It was fun for both of us, more a dalliance than a grand affair.

I set out to enjoy life to the full, and I think I did so. I had no thought of an afterlife then, any more than I do now. It took courage and daring to live as I did, to shrug off the scandals that threatened me at every turn, to care nothing for what the future might bring. When I was a young woman,

I never dreamed I would grow old, and I never considered the future. Only the present mattered. And even when those years had gone, I didn't renounce my past, but rather enveloped myself in it, like a comfortable blanket against the frost of age. Nor did I, at any time, feel the slightest twinge of guilt. In a way I pitied poor Casteltown, but I never regretted anything I had done . . .

Only in my hearts of hearts I could not bear the shame of growing old. The attentions I received from men began to dwindle, and this was inexpressibly painful. I was like a house that had formerly overflowed with guests, left empty and darkened. I began to hide from the world, and as my appearances grew rarer they were more and more carefully managed. I wore veils, I selected the hours when the light would be sufficiently dim to mask the ravages of time. Finally, only my husband remained to flatter me on my youth and beauty. He still found me utterly desirable, but for me he was the only man I could not desire. Casteltown was sincere: but the more he smothered me with his attentions, the more he reminded me of my failing power.

The compliments of other women became double-edged, as women's compliments will, and though the men who came to Doneraile were as flirtatious as ever, they did it purely out of habit. The younger ones tortured me unwittingly, for I could see in their eyes that I was no longer an attractive woman but a curiosity, a freak.

In the end, flouting convention as I always did, I moved into this top-floor room, which harbored so many sweet memories. Here at least I felt safe from prying eyes. Then I fell ill, which maddened me. In my arrogance, I considered sickness intolerable, a curse afflicting the weak and puny. I had no desire to grow old, but I was in no rush to die, either. Nevertheless I gathered myself to face the final moment without flinching.

As that moment neared, I drove everyone away from me: the doctor, who had failed to cure me, and the priest I didn't need. Throughout my life I had asked what I wanted directly of God, and he had given to me in abundance. Now that his blessings had dried up, I would not crawl to him through an intercessor.

I therefore quitted the world in a blaze of anger and bitterness, eaten up by age, infirmity, and decay. I died in the conviction that death was the ultimate disgrace.

My fury condemned me, and after my failure to pass into the light it was directed straight at my poor husband. My death grieved him beyond endurance, and I hated him for surviving me. But soon the force of my hatred slackened, and when he died his ghost came to haunt Doneraile, moaning its sorrow and its eternal love for me.

In this dimension, I am free again to do as I wish. Nothing here is ordained in advance, and there is no authority to encumber my actions. I know there is something which eludes me, and when I find it my destiny will change. What will

that be? I have no idea. I am neither happy nor unhappy. I merely lack. My present state is close to the Limbo of the Christians. It's not a crowded place, nor yet a vacuum. There is no pain, only complete neutrality.

I am alone, yet not alone, in the sense that I am aware of the millions upon millions of other waiting souls around me. I have no contact with them, as I do with you. They are vague, anonymous shapes. I cannot make out their features. But I know there is one faculty we all share: we can see into the hearts of the living, we can penetrate their deepest intimacy. The living are like open books, whose pages are steadily turning before our eyes. Their every thought, act, and feeling are perceptible to us. But they have nothing to fear, for the dead pass no judgment on what they do. They are content to observe.

At my death, I saw my lifetime repeated in every detail, and the memory of it haunts me. Far more than I haunt this house, I am myself haunted. Even now, I hide my wrinkled face behind a veil of mist. When I appeared to Geraldine in the glass, the vision was so fleeting that she thought she had glimpsed a woman as lovely as the Mother of God herself. Don't mourn me, don't despise me, don't admire me. Only imagine how I am . . . I am a young and beautiful girl.

Had Lady Casteltown told me the whole truth?

She was very convincing, but I wondered

if age and the forfeit of pleasure were really sufficient to explain her self-imposed incarceration. Her portrait in the hall at Doneraile shows a very desirable woman, despite the white hair and the wrinkles. So why did she lock herself away?

At first I suspected some kind of disfiguring illness. I put the question to Arthur Montgomery, who consulted the archives on my behalf. He returned with the news that I was quite right; Lady Casteltown apparently had, after all, a very good reason for moving to an isolated bedroom. He had turned up a letter to Lord Casteltown from an estate employee, which ended: *"We also extend our warmest and sincerest congratulations to Her Ladyship, on her complete recovery following the recent deplorable mishap."*

We had taken a major step forward, but still the whole truth eluded me. Arthur Montgomery probed further, and eventually produced the final link in the chain. It transpired that Lady Casteltown was injured in a shooting accident. She lost one eye, and thereafter had been obliged to wear a black patch to hide its gaping socket.

This, then, was the explanation. Her beauty had been cruelly marred, and in consequence she had hidden herself away, only appearing on rare occasions, heavily veiled. And Lady Casteltown's vanity pursued her beyond the grave; for even in the midst of her confession, she sought to shroud her disfigurement so that men would remember nothing but the image of her radiant loveliness.

THE GREEN AND GRAY DRESS

Gojim, Province of Porto, Portugal

THE TWO COUNTESSES OF VILLA Flore, Maria Luisa and Marie José, received Justin and myself for lunch at their palace on the ramparts of St. George's Castle, in the heart of old Lisbon. The sisters were both hale and hearty grandmothers, the very image of liveliness and hospitality. They had lived active lives, participating fully in the upheavals of their time, yet they maintained the high style of a vanished era.

About twenty representatives of the Portuguese aristocracy were seated at the long table, which glittered with silver. The superabundant fare, the quality of the wine, the numerous and attentive staff belonged to another age. While we admired the view of Lisbon's many bell towers, the Praça do Commercio (which I think is the most beautiful square on earth), and the gleaming Tagus, we talked energetically of ghosts. Apparently the countesses owned a quinta (country estate) where they swarmed like bees.

The following day we drove north, following the freeway to Aveiro before turning right into a wilder, more mountainous region. After Lamego, the valleys grew deeper, the hills taller, and the villages more sparse. The road became tortuous and narrow. We found ourselves in a country of vines and orchards, a step aside from the rest

of the world. Finally we mounted to the little village of Gojim, where the massive
boulders of granite, perfectly jointed together despite their irregular shapes, reminded
us strangely of the foundations of Inca tem-
ples. The site exhaled a sense of something
extraordinarily ancient, as if millennia had
accumulated here without effecting the
slightest change.

The quinta, which dated from the eighteenth century, was an illustration of the
province's robust Baroque style of architec-
ture. All the more touching were its rustic
attempts at elegance, in the form of vases,
pilasters, masks eaten away by time, foun-
tains, balustrades, and coats of arms.

The countesses had cast aside their smart
clothes of yesterday and now wore more
comfortable outfits. They briskly showed us
around the house. The rooms had low ceilings, and the corridors were punctuated by
dark recesses. Souvenirs brought home by
ancestors and charming old-fashioned objects
softened the furnishings, which were otherwise austere. One sensed that masters, servants, and domestic animals had always lived
here in a bundle, as tight as it was tranquil.

Our hostesses went through the inventory
of the resident wraiths. Both were refined
and artful talkers, and they knew exactly
how to conjure up these shadows from the
past.

First came the bedroom of the procurator,
who at one time was entrusted with the family's business affairs. The countesses' grandfather had long sought a reliable man to live
in the quinta, but nobody wanted the job
because the place was so famously haunted.
Finally the count unearthed a man living a
few miles from Gojim who seemed stouter
than the rest; at any rate he brandished his
pistols ferociously and declared that if any
ghost fooled with him he would give it
something to think about.

The man was engaged directly and
entrusted with the management of the quinta, with a commission to spend two or three
nights a week at the house. At that time
there was no scarcity of servants, the house
was maintained even better than today (if
that is possible), and the door hinges were
kept thoroughly oiled.

On his first night the procurator was suddenly awakened by the heavy creaking of a
door. He sensed, rather than saw, a shadow
cross the threshold and approach him.

"Who's that?" he roared.

No answer. The shadow moved inexorably
forward, so the procurator reached for his
pistol and let fly. But this did not halt the
apparition. The procurator fired a second
shot, and would have fired a third, had his
pistol not jammed.

Now the shadow was over him, bent

above him. He lashed out with his fists, which sank into some soft substance, a substance which was not human flesh, which pressed on him and seemed to suffocate. He tried to light a candle but his shaking hand could find no matches. The pressure increased inexorably. Finally, he shrieked, "Stop! Stop! Stop!" and the shadow let out a snarl like a wounded beast.

At last the man writhed free and rolled off the bed. He staggered outside, mounted his horse, and galloped the several miles that separated him from his home village, where he arrived at about four in the morning. He hammered on the shutters like a madman till his sons opened the door; then, after gasping out his story, he retired to bed and fell asleep.

Next morning the procurator failed to appear for breakfast, and the sons left him to sleep in peace. Eleven o'clock passed, then noon. At about one they went to wake him. They found their father's body rolled up in the covers, stone dead.

The story ran across the province like wildfire, and the house in Gojim was shunned thereafter, as a place that harbored a ghost which could do murder.

Countess Marie José now took the lead. We followed her down to the sunny courtyard with its plump round paving stones, and out to the lane which ran between the quinta and an orchard carpeted with chamomile. Here we found ourselves facing a ground-floor window entirely framed in heavy granite. Behind this was the bedroom of Father Joachim, formerly the quinta's private chaplain.

Father Joachim (said Marie José) was no faintheart. After the 1910 revolution against the church and the monarchy, he refused point-blank to wear laymen's clothes, like so many of his less robust colleagues. "If anyone doesn't like it," he declared, "let them say so: and we shall see what happens." Every Saturday evening, he went up to the quinta for the night, and was ready next morning to say the weekly mass. The day came, however, when he informed the old count that henceforth he would forgo his Saturday night's lodging, and toil up from the village on Sunday morning instead.

Why?

At first he refused to say, but in the end the truth came out. Latterly he had awoken from a deep sleep in his room to hear a voice calling clear as a bell: "Father Joachim! Father Joachim!" Thinking he was needed to give some poor soul the last rites, he hurried to the window. Outside, the road was drenched with moonlight but completely deserted. Perhaps the voice belonged to somebody within the house? He opened the bedroom door, but the corridors and salons were as empty as the road. Then he heard the voice again, in the distance: "Father Joachim! Father Joachim!" and he concluded that whoever was searching for him had gone to the village church.

Father Joachim was frozen now, and he felt old and tired; pushing the incident out of his mind, he climbed stiffly back into bed. Scarcely had he closed his eyes when right beside him the same voice spoke again, this time loudly and spitefully. Crushed with remorse, Father Joachim dressed and went to the chapel, where he spent the rest of the night in prayer: and never again would he agree to spend the night at the quinta.

I asked the two countesses about their own experiences with ghosts, which they both proceeded to recount with relish. Countess Marie José remembered that when she was fourteen she was put to sleep in the haunted bedroom with her governess. One night she woke up with a sensation of icy cold, as if snow had billowed into the room. A shadowy figure swayed beside the bed. It seemed to be a woman, but she was unable (as usual with ghosts) to make out its face; and it was covered from head to toe with a dark, gownlike garment, such as Venetians wear at Carnival. Shivering with cold and fright, Marie José asked her bedmate if she too could see the figure. The governess re-

turned no answer, but the sound of her chattering teeth was as good as an affirmation.

"What do you want?" whispered Marie José to the apparition. Silence: the cold intensified, and in spite of herself Marie José began to pray. At this the shadow backed away, opened the door, and went out, as soundlessly as it had entered.

Both countesses agreed that on other occasions they had heard sundry heavy footfalls in the corridor outside their bedrooms; but surprisingly enough they were still resolutely skeptical. "We think these things are no more than dreams and exaggeration," they told me, in all sincerity.

Perhaps their skepticism served as a defense against real fear, to ward off forces of the kind they had faced six or seven years earlier.

One night, when they were both sleeping in the bedroom next to their father's—the old gentleman was still alive at that time—they were awakened by a rumbling sound which appeared to come from beneath the bed. It increased so quickly in volume that they began to think an earthquake was under way, earthquakes being not uncommon in Portugal.

The rumbling continued for a few minutes, then abruptly ceased, whereupon the two women rushed into the bedroom of their father, whom they found asleep. He had

heard nothing, and neither had the servants.

I found these stories very impressive, and yet nothing about the huge old building struck me as particularly sinister. On the contrary, there was something delicious and elderly about it, a vague, quiet poetry and charm tempered by melancholy. Of course I detected ghosts, several of them, but the atmosphere suggested nothing malign or aggressive or macabre.

Having exhausted the topic of ghosts, our hosts fell back on their ancestors, as aristocrats will. Theirs had belonged to the courts of successive Portuguese monarchs and had taken a firsthand part in their country's turbulent history. They had known—and survived—mad queens, black conspiracies, kings who vanished mysteriously, foreign invasions, banishments, and the nasty caprices of tyrannical Infantas.

The nineteenth century brought the family to the forefront of history, when Portugal was ravaged by a bloody civil war. Maria da Gloria, the beautiful and courageous young queen who was the champion of the liberals, was fighting to keep the throne that her own uncle, the formidable Dom Miguel, was seeking to steal from her, with the support of the conservative section of the nobility. In this fight the ancestor of my countesses, the first Count Samodaes, rallied to the cause of the royal heroine. He won battle after battle

as Maria's general-in-chief, and thanks to him Dom Miguel was driven into exile, leaving Maria da Gloria sole mistress of Portugal.

The years passed, and Samodaes grew old. He and his wife made a joint will, in which they made clear their desire to be buried in the private chapel of their favorite property, the quinta at Gojim.

They overlooked the fact that a law had recently been promulgated in Portugal forbidding all burials outside cemeteries.

When they died, their only son and heir found himself in a quandary. Should he betray the last will of his parents, or break the law? Fortunately, the second Count Samodaes was a powerful man. As a councillor to the king, a peer of the realm, and a talented writer with friendships in both the intellectual and political milieux, he won the authorities' permission to inter his parents in the family chapel, but "in silence, secretly, and during the hours of darkness."

Up hill and down dale, the funeral cortege plodded onward through the night. The coaches had to halt in the valley, because at that time there were no paved roads leading into the steep mountains overlooking the River Douro. But the count and his wife had brought with them a few of their most trusted servants, and these carried torches to light the way for the two horses bearing the

coffins as they journeyed on into the hills.

After a six-day march, they reached the walls of Gojim a little after midnight. At the house, the servants and farm workers were sleeping soundly. The travelers slipped through the gates of the quinta and crossed the courtyard as quietly as they could. After manhandling the coffins through the narrow doorway of the chapel, they lit their lamps and moved aside the heavy granite slab which sealed the family vault.

The servants who had carried the coffins were dog-tired and it was a great effort for them to move the huge stone and make an opening of sufficient width. Finally, they lowered the two coffins into the vault; after which they retired to bed, unable to muster the strength to replace the stone.

Only the young count and countess kept silent vigil before the gaping aperture. For hours they stood like this, until at last the sallow light of dawn drove the shadows from the chapel; at which time they crossed themselves and retired to bed in their turn. Thus it was that the young Countess Samodaes spent her first night at her beloved Quinta de Gojim—beside a coffin.

"Look, here is her portrait," said Maria Luisa.

We were in one of the corner salons. The ceiling here was richly decorated with frescoes, higher than in the other rooms of the house; the walls were covered with portraits of ancestors. I started when I saw the one Maria Luisa had indicated.

"Do you remember," I said to her sister, "do you remember what I told you yesterday in Lisbon, while we were having lunch?"

It was toward the end of the meal, and the conversation was flowing along in lively fashion. I was chatting of this and that with Marie José when I detected an image sliding between us. I could still see the room around me and the other guests, but it was as if a kind of fine fabric had swirled across the scene. I identified a gray skirt, probably of silk, cut in the romantic style of the last century. Two fringes of green silk appeared to frame the skirt. I had no idea what this vision meant, but when I saw it I immediately described it to Marie José. And now here I was at Gojim, looking at the portrait of a woman wearing the same skirt, of the same color, framed by the two ends of a green silk shawl. The figure was attractive and energetic in demeanor, with eyes that brimmed with appeal. I read the name: "Doña Henriqueta Adelaide Vieira de Magalhaes, Countess of Samodaes."

Burning to know more, I interrogated Maria Luisa, who seemed to have all the facts at her fingertips. Though a considerable flirt, Doña Henriqueta had remained entirely faithful to her husband. She was fond of clothes and delighted in exactly the kind of *mondain* amusements that her shy and intellectual husband shunned. But the countess took no notice and continued to parade around the city of Porto, her fief, in her splendid four-in-hand.

A countess, a millionairess, and a peerless letter writer, this remarkable woman was excellent ghost material. The only trouble was she had spent very little time at Gojim. She had scant reason for haunting the place, and she hadn't even died there; and according to Marie José, if there was a female specter in the vicinity, it was certainly not Henriqueta's. Her vote went to Josephina, another ancestress whose portrait hung in the salon. Yet my strange glimpse of Countess Henriqueta's dress had nothing to do with chance, and following my intuition I asked to be shown the chapel, in the conviction that it contained something that might be of great interest to me.

Once again we crossed the sunny courtyard, this time to enter the side door of the church. Its stark simplicity was offset by a raised, richly decorated altar. There was the usual blend of religious images and paper flowers, along with a faint odor of candlewax. In the center of the granite floor was the broad stone slab beneath which the lords of Gojim slumbered.

Here the first Count Samodaes had been surreptitiously interred. I was certain that his daughter-in-law, the lady in the portrait, was there too, and I said so to Marie José. She was categorical: there was no way that this particular ancestress could possibly be here. But her sister was more circumspect. "I've been in the vault myself," she said. "I was about eleven or twelve. My father had it opened and I asked if I could go in with him. He never could refuse me anything. . . . We climbed down a rickety old ladder. I can remember bones, plenty of them, because most of the coffins had moldered away. I can't remember seeing more than two or three intact, and I can't remember if Henriqueta's was among them. The vault hasn't been reopened since."

Despite this disappointing information, the coolness and calm in the chapel invited me to remain there . . . alone. The two countesses were gracious enough to allow this and quietly retired, closing the low door behind them. For a long moment silence reigned, while my memory reconstituted the image of Henriqueta.

I am the woman in the portrait. Only, the gray dress was really a blue one. The painting has faded with age and the fabric has changed color . . . I am buried under the floor of this chapel, because this was my husband's favorite house. I wanted to rest with him here. If I haunt these surroundings, which I visited so seldom in my lifetime, it is because the magnificent and terrible secret which has reduced me to ghosthood is closely linked to Gojim. But until now nobody has seen or felt my presence, because I do not wish it.

I came from a great sunny seaport, full of life and movement, with ships constantly coming and going. I grew up to the cries of sailors echoing up the alleys, shouted orders, the rumbling of over-loaded wagons; and the scent of wine was every-where, for we lived in a vineyard region and the warehouses where the great barrels were stored were close beside our house.

Then I was married, and very happily. I adored my husband and I think he adored me. He was a deep one, a melancholy man, though it is possible to be a thinking, shy person without being sad to boot. Sometimes, when he looked at me, I felt his eyes belonged to someone else, to someone filled with compassion and immeasurable sorrow.

I loved a joke, I loved fun, I loved laughter. Laughter for me was like spring sunshine. I was pretty, too. Pretty! I attracted men, but I would go no further. I loved pretty things, elegant car-riages, beautiful furniture and jewelry. I loved to handle fine cloths, too, and I spent hours choosing them. The peddlers who traveled from town to town, and from great house to great house, knew that they could always make a sale to me. I pre-ferred light fabrics, and I even wore them up here at Gojim, in the harsh mountain weather. I loved

to hear the rustle of warm silk against rough granite. The pale blue in my portrait (which has turned to gray) was my favorite color; a very soft blue, which God has used for certain flowers of spring.

My husband chided me for frivolity, but I believe he was quietly proud of my position in the town. I wasn't at all vain about it myself. In my own eyes, I was no more than a woman people admired, perhaps envied, sometimes courted. Other men didn't interest me. Every day I spent several hours working at my correspondence. My letters had a certain success, they were read aloud and applauded at dinner parties. Today they are for-gotten, filed away in some moldering archive.

In town, I had a household to run, parties to attend, a family to take care of, and a large for-tune to manage. All this filled up my days. I did not spend enough time with my husband, which we both regretted. So when we came to Gojim together it was with the deepest pleasure. Even though my first experience here was utterly lugubrious, I grew to love the place, because here I could be alone with my husband and my children.

We went for long rides around the district. We left early in the morning, giving ourselves ample time, because we never knew how many hours we would be out. We rode local horses, accustomed to the terrain. When we reached the mountaintops we viewed the landscape stretching away to the horizon, and the smoke of the peasants' fires rising straight into the still sky. The sweet smell of woodsmoke was everywhere. Often we went to the Hermitage of Our Lady, far away in the hills. I made those trips last as long as possible, for always I felt a strange unwillingness to go home at the end of the day.

I was happy, yet something troubled me. It seemed to me that I was being kept in ignorance about the quinta. At first I wondered if my husband was hiding something about its history, but I rapidly concluded that this was out of the question. Perhaps the factor, or the bailiff, or even some member of my husband's family? This too seemed highly unlikely. The vague discomfort persisted, until I realized that the mystery was contained in the house itself. How much did the others know? I couldn't question them, because I had no idea where to start.

One day my husband and I were alone together in the library. The room was a small one, and in it the various documents relevant to the quinta were stored on shelves—things like ledgers, title deeds, and reports. They were all bound together in fat volumes which in some sort made up a daily journal of the estate's progress. And while my husband was looking for a document, one of these volumes fell to the floor, releasing a sheet of white paper. I picked it up, unfolded it, and began to read.

The script was full and sloping, with fine flourishes. When I had finished I passed it without a word to my husband, who read it in turn, then silently looked me full in the eyes. Both our faces were sheet-white.

There are secrets of this planet which naturally belong to the soil; and there are secrets which human beings have buried deep, which lie undiscovered by their descendants. The one we had chanced upon belonged to the latter category: and it was a very terrible one. I cannot say more . . . only that it was a great treasure, but not of the kind that arouses human greed. It was not gold, nor any precious stone . . .

In antiquity there existed on the borders of India and Persia a tribe which founded a curious cult, based on a blend of mysticism and depravity. Their rituals, conducted in caves, involved sacrifices, prayers, and dances centered on roughly carved altars, culminating with a sex act, which the officiating priests performed among themselves. The cult also possessed a spiritual treasure of fabulous antiquity and enormous significance, whose physical appearance it was forbidden to describe. In one of the caves the members of the cult had come upon something which constituted an important element of knowledge, concerning a dimension that was normally inaccessible to human beings; and they concluded that this thing had to remain in concealment until a being capable of deciphering it should appear. The guardians understood the value of what they had in charge, to the point that they would give their lives to preserve it; yet at the

same time they had no access to its meaning. Metaphorically speaking, they were like sentinels guarding a safe to which they did not possess the combination.

Because of their religious practices, the members of the cult were hounded from their country of origin. They came here, bringing with them their treasure; and their choice of this area was a deliberate one. In truth, everything is the fruit of calculation, not of chance, even though human beings cannot grasp the workings of the force which directs what they only see as randomness and coincidence.

Long ago, this corner of the Portuguese hills was utterly cut off from the rest of the world, and because of this it rated as a perfect sanctuary. Moreover, the land harbored an elemental sexual energy which suited the cult's ritual practices very well. To this day, things go on behind the thick granite walls of this village which would make your hair stand on end. If you could see through these old stones, you would discover a complete repertoire of erotic fantasy. The fact is that this sleepy village high in the hills of Portugal is built on a center of sexual power comparable to the great sanctuaries of Delos or Ephesus.

The members of the cult built a temple here, whose vestiges lie beneath the quinta and in its immediate vicinity. After several generations, they and their religion died out, and their houses and their sanctuary disappeared. Many centuries later other men came to occupy the site and till the land,

culminating with the construction of a great noble house.

Eventually the newcomers stumbled on the treasure of the cult which had formerly lived here. They had sufficient insight to guess that it embodied some prodigious spiritual truth, though they were unable to penetrate its workings or its significance. So they too became its uncomprehending guardians, realizing that it was wisest to preserve the secret intact.

Who were these guardians? They were local people whose best protection was their peasant taciturnity. The consequence was a kind of secret society which watched over the treasure from generation to generation.

At length this society threw up a member who attained a higher level of education than his fellows, having risen from his peasant condition to become a clerk working for the estate. With his smattering of culture, he lost the deep awe of the ancient treasure maintained by his fellows. It was not that he meant to make use of it, only that in contrast to the others, who were its servants, he thought himself its master. And he was guilty of an unpardonable act, that of revealing the identity and existence of the treasure on a single sheet of paper. He died soon after, the victim of a horrible accident.

But his sheet of paper remained, hidden in one of the registers in the quinta's library where the man had worked. And there, by chance, my husband and I stumbled upon it.

My husband enjoined me to absolute secrecy, and I kept my word to him. But my curiosity was too great. I wanted to discover the meaning of the treasure. As I said before, it was like a safe whose combination had been lost: and I was fool enough to try to force it open. The treasure immediately vanished into thin air, because it incorporated an intellectual mechanism which caused it to destroy itself if an unqualified mind attempted to tamper with it. And that was the end of it.

Soon afterwards I died of a very ordinary sickness, which also carried away many of my contemporaries. Nobody was particularly surprised by this, but to my certain knowledge it was the automatic consequence of my act. The secret I had tried to violate had the power to destroy its desecrator, and moreover it condemned me to my present condition. What I had done unleashed an energy which constrained me at the instant of my death.

And ever since I have watched and listened, learning much. Ghosts are by no means perfect; the very fact that we have failed to rise into the light is the proof of it. This shred of ourselves which remains behind retains the qualities and the faults we possessed when we were flesh and blood. Nevertheless we are influenced by the knowledge we acquire after our death, and above all, by the goal that is set for us to attain. Since my death I have kept vigil over my descendants and over this house that I loved so much. Despite the atmosphere of sadness it exudes, this will always be a place of peace, and our family will continue to live here in tranquillity for generations to come.

N.B.: My eminent Iranian friend, Ahmad Ali S.A., has confirmed the existence in Eastern Iran of religious brotherhoods exclusively confined to males, whose origins go back to the pre-Aryan epoch.

THE WHIM OF DESTINY

Iuelsberg Castle, Fyn Island, Denmark

J USTIN AND I HAD ARRIVED ON FYN the day before. With its undulating meadows of green and yellow, its woods and comely manor houses, its white northern Gothic churches overlooking thatched, half-timbered villages bright with lilac, gorse, and flowering may, the last thing you would expect on this big smiling island was a ghost. As we drove across it, I felt more and more like Daudet's *sous-préfet au champ*, and a wild notion possessed me to drop my work, tear off my suit, stretch my length in the grass, and write reams of bad verse.

Yet, I told myself, this clean, vivid, beautifully kept Denmark contains one of the most famous ghosts of history, that of Hamlet's father.

Invigorated by the brisk Danish spring, we left Nyborg and drove several miles north, before turning off along a tremendous avenue of old oaks. After this the road traversed a wood and passed in front of a large nineteenth-century farmhouse, before entering a private park. Here the meadows sloped gently to the shores of artificial lakes carefully bordered by copses. An intricately wrought metal gate appeared alongside the drive, opening on a garden à la française, where every lawn edge was marked straight as a bowstring. In the background loomed the long facade of Iuelsberg Castle, built in

the eighteenth century in an austere and solid Baroque style bereft of putti, vases, volutes, and suchlike fripperies.

We had arranged a rendezvous with the Weeping Girl, whose melancholy name had enticed me from Paris in a fever to know more about her. But the owner of the house, Erik Iuel, speedily took the wind from my sails.

"There has never been any weeping girl here," he declared gravely. "It's a total invention."

Catastrophe. We were sitting in the huge, bright kitchen of the castle, in which period furniture rubbed shoulders companionably with the ovens and dishwashers. I stared gloomily into my coffee cup. If there was no ghost, then I had made this trip for nothing. All I could do was accept the offer of a guided tour of the house before going straight home again.

The sheer quality of the collections restored my good humor. Even if there were no ghosts here, we should at least have seen some very beautiful objects by the time we took our leave. The family portraits were of a uniformly high standard, and those of the kings of Denmark pleasingly bizarre, the best being a profile of the dynasty's hero, Christian IV, with his hair knotted into a long pigtail culminating in an enormous pearl. The porcelain came from the very best

makers, and the furniture shimmered with sophisticated marquetry. A particular treasure was the magnificent Savonnerie tapestry commissioned by Louis XIV, which was straight out of the Hall of Mirrors at Versailles. These marvels combined to banish all thought of ghost-hunting from my mind.

On the bend of a broad staircase, Erik Iuel showed me a painting of a highly elaborate castle. This, he said, was Iuelsberg before his family acquired it in 1770; in other words, before they replaced it with a larger residence in the style of the period and laid out an English garden to replace the Italian one. At the far end of a corridor reserved for guests, we entered a corner bedroom decorated with mahogany furniture and chintz fabrics. And at this point, to my complete surprise, Erik Iuel began to tell me a very curious story.

Erik's brother, an eccentric, complicated, artistic character, had died ten years previously. One day Erik happened to be listening to a cassette of Leonard Cohen that had once belonged to his brother. Suddenly the song was interrupted and Erik heard the wail of a child, followed by the cries of seagulls. Then he started as he recognized two familiar voices, those of his father and his brother, both of whom were dead. They were discussing ghosts, and Erik's father was telling of an experience in the room in which we now found ourselves.

"One night, I was woken from a deep sleep by an unfamiliar sensation. I had the conviction that something, or someone, was in the room with me. I tried to penetrate the darkness, and before long I distinguished the indistinct outlines of a looming black shadow. I wondered at first if some large bird had entered the room, but no bird could be that large. I got up and checked the window, which was closed: nothing could have come in that way. And when I turned round the shadow had faded away. I looked at my watch—it was two o'clock in the morning."

Erik Iuel now showed himself quite clear on one point. His father had been far too stiff a man ever to indulge in a discussion of such nonsense as ghosts, and would never in life have allowed his views on the matter to be recorded. Yet here was a voice to prove the contrary, and what was more it went on to relate a second ghost story. Apparently Count B., the head of one of Denmark's greatest families and a regular guest of the Iuels, was habitually lodged in the corner bedroom—until the day when he announced that for nothing in the world would he ever sleep there again. At exactly two in the morning he invariably found himself awoken by an invisible but extraordinarily powerful presence. It happened, however, that his

wish was overlooked, and the next time he came he was given the same bedroom. Next day, when the chambermaid brought up breakfast, she found in the bed not Count, but Countess B., his wife, who was not so impressionable.

We visited the other guest bedrooms, which were all decorated simply and gaily. There were no communicating doors, yet I had a distinct impression that they were originally designed to lead into one another. Erik Iuel confirmed this: all the doors had been walled up in the last century.

The last chamber was that normally occupied by Erik's sister. Although the furniture here was far from old, there was a distinctly romantic air about this room. In one corner stood a full-length looking glass with a bronze frame. I contemplated this, wondering who, in the more or less distant past, had examined their reflection here; for I had a fleeting impression that somebody, a woman, was on the point of making her appearance. The little desk by the window especially attracted me, and I sat down at it, feeling a strong temptation to take up a pen and write.

I raised my eyes and took in the view across the park. The tall trees on the lawn had been positioned with careful artlessness, and the grass stretched away to the foot of a neoclassical pavilion sited among rocks. I found this pavilion with its fringe of old beeches singularly attractive; I could not take my eyes off it.

Along the walls of the room next door ran shelf after shelf of old volumes with gold-titled calfskin bindings. In the middle was a massive billiard table, which didn't look as if it was used very often. The library was spacious and airy, but for some reason it seemed thoroughly oppressive to me: worst of all, it chilled me to the bone. The temperature was several degrees lower here than in the other rooms. Erik Iuel acknowledged that his sister was frightened by the billiard room and did her best to avoid going there. He often teased her about this when they were children; one of his evil tricks was to leave a hundred-krone note in the middle of the billiard table which she could have for herself if she collected it before dawn. She invariably did so, because she badly needed money, but the effort scared her half to death. She was quite right, I thought . . .

The billiard table had a drawer in which the various ivory balls were kept. Every night, Erik's sister heard the dry rumble and crack of these balls shifting about in this drawer, and as soon as this happened she would leap out of bed, open the communicating door, and switch on the light. There was never anybody in the room, and the billiard-ball drawer was always firmly shut.

I heartily shared the views of Erik's sister, and preferred to remain alone in her former bedroom. My glance traveled from the cheval glass to the little desk in front of the window, and a portrait slowly fastened itself onto my brain.

It was the image of a young woman of the Romantic period. Dark-eyed, with a pretty face and a mischievous mouth, she carried her head gracefully and wore a blue dress. The only thing was that the image was that of a Spanish girl, about as far from a Danish ghost as it was possible to be. Despite my best efforts, I could not prize the creature out of my mind.

I was born in this bedroom. Almost immediately we had to leave the house, and it was not until much later that I returned here and remained a virtual prisoner on the premises for many years. I wasn't locked away by some jealous husband or envious brother: I was a voluntary recluse.

At a very early age I was gripped by a passion for writing. We didn't go to school; instead tutors were brought from Copenhagen to give lessons to me and to my brothers and sisters. I always liked composition best and I excelled at it. By the time I was ten my writings were being read aloud at family gatherings. I was too young to be there myself, but I listened at the door and swelled with pride at the things that were said about me.

As a teenager, I wrote poetry which I dedicated

to my parents, my grandparents, and the other people I loved. And to him. He was my cousin, with whom I fell madly in love at the age of fifteen. He lived in a castle on another island and every summer he came with his family to spend the summer season here. He was a couple of years older than I was and he had a pale face and very dark eyes. With his unruly hair he seemed to me the very personification of romance. But his nature was ill-assorted to his looks, for his temperament was dull and his mind devoid of sparkle. He was destined not for adventure, tragedy, and passion, but to become a great plodding magnate and the founder of a dynasty. Yet there was no reason why the two of us should not marry, because my own family and fortune placed us in the same rank of society.

One evening before dinner, I declared my love for him in a poem which I slid under his plate. He saw the piece of paper, read it, folded it, and slipped it in his pocket. At the far end of the table I sat trembling, burning to know what his reaction would be. But he said not a word, either then or later. I did the same thing again and again, sending poem after poem, none of which elicited any more response than the first. But instead of running away from me, he remained constantly at my side. I dared not ask him what he felt about me, and for his part he continued mute: yet I often saw his big dark eyes contemplating me, and I thought I could see love in them.

One day I fell ill. The sickness was a creeping one, which slowly gnawed at the muscles of my legs, until I lost the use of them. Unable to move, I had to be carried about everywhere, and a special wheelchair was constructed for me. From the start I knew my days were numbered but I was so young that I felt sure I still had time enough ahead of me. I knew one thing: I wished to pass out of the world from the place where I had entered it. So I moved into this bedroom.

I so often looked at myself in the big cheval mirror that if a person stared at it for long enough today they might see my face appear. There would be my small pink mouth, my straight nose, and my dark, shining, joyous eyes. I closely resembled one of my contemporaries, whose portrait is now exhibited in Madrid.

I often wore a blue dress with a white collar, which turned into a kind of uniform for me. Clad like this, I lingered for hours at the little desk in front of the window. Writing was my passion; I covered page after page. From time to time I would raise my eyes and gaze out at the white pavilion on the far side of the park; it seemed to me that my muse lived there, and she spent her time busily recharging my imagination. Despite my illness I experienced moments of great happiness in this room, though even in my lifetime it had begun to accumulate the residue of melancholy which it has retained ever since. This may be on account of the ghost who inhabits the library next door. Something horrible must have happened there, for even in my lifetime I was aware of the room's icy *coldness and seldom allowed myself to be carried through it.*

When I was twenty-five, my handsome cousin was married. I was invited to the wedding but I didn't go. He went away to live on his estates— or rather his new wife's estates—and never returned to Iuelsberg. I never saw him again, but his image continued to obsess me, and from that creature of ordinary flesh and blood I fashioned a superman, the harbinger of all virtue and talent. Everything I wrote was for him, though I did so in such a way that no one could possibly have recognized him. Each one of my verses transfigured the object of my impossible love, which had been rendered impossible by my sickness.

Gradually I became convinced that I would die young. What counted most was not that I should prolong my life for a few more years, but that I should be given time enough to encapsulate my destiny in a work of great art.

I published a limited edition of my poems, which caused a sensation in society and in literary circles. The illness from which I was known to suffer, my reputation as a beauty, and the talent attributed to me brought the success which was to destroy me.

People started coming here. I held court in my bedroom, and in another specially fitted salon on the second floor. Soon I became so plagued by visitors that I began to cast about for a refuge where I could write in peace. I thought of the columned pavilion I could see from my room, and had myself wheeled up there in my chair. Inside, it consisted of a large white-painted room, furnished with pinewood tables and armchairs. There were six big windows and a view across the countryside. It was perfect for my needs, and thereafter I went there every day with the pretty, bronze-encrusted mahogany escritoire, made in England, in which I kept my inkpot, my pens, and my thick, cream-colored sheets of paper.

Nobody ever came to disturb me at the pavilion.

As time went by, the illness wasted and aged my body more and more, though my ability to write was preserved intact. My condition fluctuated with the seasons, which transformed the countryside around my pavilion, while my will to create blossomed in inverse proportion. The muse of my first attempts at poetry was pushed aside by an angel. I know I was near death, and although I was anything but frightened, death began to gain the ascendant in my writings as well as in my body. Little by little, page by page, its presence overshadowed every word I set down.

I published a collection of essays, blending lyricism and metaphysics with the alchemy of my own experience. The success of this book enlarged my circle of readers and the trickle of visitors grew to a flood. Largely by word of mouth, I had become a major object of curiosity. Sometimes my admirers wrote to ask for a meeting, but more often they just appeared at the door in elegant carriages

drawn by pairs of horses, or having walked or ridden for several days. I received them patiently in one or other of my two rooms. Mostly they came to learn more about death, which by force of circumstance had become my principal subject matter. I explained my view that death was no more than a state in our passage to a much better state of being.

The interest I aroused in my readers made up for my own family's lack of concern. My relatives were generous, hospitable, and open, but they were bored and baffled by all intellectual concerns. They genuinely loved me and their grief over my fate was unfeigned. They appreciated my work but scarcely understood it, and they came up to see me whenever I had no callers, that is, early in the mornings or late in the evenings, when the tide had receded. If the truth be known, my brothers and sisters were fed up with all the commotion, and ardently hoped that calm would soon be restored.

Far from cutting back on my activities, I extended them. At that time romanticism was all the rage, and Denmark offered broad cultural refinements along with an intense intellectual life represented by good writers, novelists, poets, and playwrights. All of these people knew each other and kept in close touch. I kept up detailed correspondences even with those I had not met. I spent days crouched over my escritoire, communicating furiously with clouds of new friends, groups, and literary circles. Through my unseen correspondents

I was able to reach places that were unknown to me, and distant houses I would never visit. For by this time I could barely move at all.

The daily meetings in my room, the literary talk and work, and the correspondence overshadowed by death somehow diverted my attention from the imminence of my own end. Yet from time to time the thought rose to the surface of my mind. Sometimes I was able to face the prospect with confidence and resolve. At other times I found myself shivering with horror, a horror that inhabited my inmost heart. Yet I deeply believed in the prospect of an afterlife, and I trusted that God in his mercy would bring me to this state, which I felt I had richly deserved.

One day I was invited to a castle not far from the capital, a great house that belonged to a family of aristocratic intellectuals, renowned then as now for their literary and artistic interests. A large party had been convened, and I assured myself that for me this would be a chance to savor that last and greatest of pleasures, a farewell to the world. I was barely thirty, and I knew there was no time left.

The journey was a miserable one. It rained steadily and the wind howled, despite the advent of summer. I went first by coach, then by boat, then by coach again. At my destination I was welcomed as the greatest writer in Denmark, and installed in the best room in the house. This room, on the second floor, was decorated with magnificent wall hangings and wonderfully carved boiseries, unaltered for centuries. There was also a huge cast-iron stove. All in all, my room was the museum piece of the castle, which was only used on the most special occasions.

The great soirée was a glorious success. My wheelchair was pushed through salon after salon, filled with a brilliant, animated company. The men were in tails, the women in light summer gowns. We had the latest gazettes from London, Vienna, St. Petersburg, Naples, Dresden, Frankfurt, and Leipzig, for in addition to speaking French and German, we kept ourselves fully informed about publications in English and Italian. We discussed all the most recent books, copies of which lay piled on the tables around us. All this was a delight to me.

The dinner that followed was a frivolous interlude. The dining-room windows gave onto the park where the last light of the evening lingered. The chandeliers and candelabras were reflected in the tall mirrors, and the brightness of the flowers rivaled that of the silver table settings. Meantime the conversation was light and brilliant.

Afterwards we returned to the salon and the talk once again became serious. Everyone gathered around me to listen to my views, and I delivered them with all the more conviction because I knew that I would never see these people again, that this was my last public appearance, and that I must leave the house next morning. The rapt attention of the company made me feel like a great queen holding court.

At last I was carried back to my bedroom. But I was too excited to fall asleep immediately. Tomorrow I would return home; the fatigue of the journey would certainly weaken me so much that when I finally reached my own bed, I would probably never leave it again.

Death would come, in just the way I had so often imagined it. I would lie on my back, leaning against a mound of pillows. I would wear, not a nightgown, but my favorite dress, the blue one with the white collar, and my hair would be newly done. I would sink into oblivion surrounded by a few loving relatives, in an atmosphere of calm and melancholy. Outside in the park, my readers and admirers would await my end in silent grief. A lighted candle would be placed on the windowsill, ready to be snuffed out as a signal to the waiting throngs that I was dead. By that time, my spirit would be far away. They would mourn for me, but I would already have found the light . . .

Soothed by this vision, I drifted off to sleep.

The stove in my room had been extinguished for several weeks with the coming of summer, but on that particular evening the air was cool. Because my health was so delicate, the stove had been relit; unfortunately the flue had not been properly cleaned and while I was asleep it took fire. The flames quickly spread to the tinder-dry silk hangings on the walls, and from thence to the wood paneling. By the time I awoke two sides of the room were burning fiercely. I whimpered and

tugged madly at the bell sash, but no one came. I dragged myself to the foot of the bed, only to watch helplessly as the fire licked closer and closer. Then my courage evaporated; down crashed the intricate structure I had built around the delicious idea of death, and I began to scream with naked fear of what was about to happen to me.

In that hideous moment, a kindly providence made sure that I was suffocated by smoke before I could be burned alive. At the moment of losing consciousness I saw that the curtains were aflame.

Finally the noise of the conflagration woke my hosts. They came running with their servants to find half the room burning out of control. Although the flames had not yet reached the bed, my little body was already charred and shriveled.

My final shriek of anguish tore me back from the light.

THE NAMELESS CRIMINAL

Château de Niedzica, Galicia, Poland

"IGOR, DO YOU KNOW OF AN INTEResting ghost anywhere in Poland?"

"Well," said my friend the sculptor, "as it happens, when I was a student in Warsaw I went to a haunted castle up in the mountains."

"Who was the ghost?"

"An Inca princess."

"You're joking! A real Inca princess, in this corner of Europe?"

"It's quite true. They say she was buried in a silver casket." I grinned. "I bet there was a whole subplot, with hidden treasure and all the rest of it."

"How did you know? It was an enormous hoard, which was never found . . . "

Of course I didn't believe him, but the story was interesting enough to follow up. Guided at a distance by Igor we set out on the track of this unusual ghost. Our plane landed at Kraków and from there we drove south for several hours across a carefully cultivated, undulating landscape. Then we turned southeast, and before long the horizon was broken by hills, on whose slopes grew thick woodlands alternating with meadows. In the distance rose the snowy jagged peaks of the Tartar Mountains.

I saw no townships, only the occasional hamlet frozen in time. Our road led through a romantic backward region, with a quality of fairyland; then mounted more and more steeply into the mountains until, rounding a final hairpin bend, we saw the castle of Niedzica looming ahead of us with its massive square keep and tall ramparts. Everything around it seemed so harsh and desolate that I expected at any moment to see the carriage of Count Dracula come bowling out of the trees; and indeed these were the foothills of the Carpathians which were the vampire's home.

We arrived at the castle only to discover one of the most sinister legacies of communism I had yet seen, for on the far side of the hill on which it stood, at the bottom of the valley, a monstrous dam was under construction. This had already irreparably scarred this otherwise perfect region.

However, the ugly modern world had not yet penetrated Niedzica's gates, for to enter them as evening fell was to walk straight into the past. We crossed the great irregularly shaped courtyard, partly surrounded by shadowy arcades, to where the curator, Sergiusz Michalcruk, was awaiting us.

Sergiusz told us his story with the measured smoothness of one who has told the same tale many times over. Ever since the Middle Ages, it seemed, two great fortresses had protected this section of the frontier; namely Czosztyn in Poland on the left bank of the Dunajac River, and Niedzica in Hungary on the right bank. In the course of endless wars, invasions, and partitioning, these castles passed from hand to hand, now belonging to one country, now to the other. The castle on the left bank, which remained the property of the Polish state, fell into ruins in this century; but Niedzica, having been sold to private owners, continued to prosper. For many centuries it had belonged to the Benesh family, who were prominent in the region. At the end of the eighteenth century, the head of this family was Sebastian Benesh, an enterprising character who left this quiet backwater to lead a life of adventure.

For a while Sebastian followed the profession of pirate. Little is known about this period of his life except that he became extremely rich, in record time. So rich that within a few years he was able to land in Peru (then a Spanish colony) and take for his wife an Inca princess. The couple had one daughter called Umira, and for a while they were perfectly happy together, raising their child in the fullness of their prosperity. At length Umira grew up and married one of her cousins, the Inca prince Tupaka Umaru.

Sebastian Benesh had time to witness the birth of his grandson before things began to go seriously wrong. The Indian population suddenly rose up against the Spanish occupants and there were rumors that the cause of the rebellion had to do with the ownership of a great store of treasure, perhaps the very one which the Incas had brought to Pizarro two centuries earlier, and which they had secretly removed after that ruthless scoundrel executed the Inca monarch. At all events, the Spaniards contrived to crush the revolt.

It is likely that Sebastian Benesh's family took part in this insurrection, because they suffered considerably in consequence of the Indian defeat. Nothing more was ever heard of Sebastian's wife, but he and his daughter, Umira, his son-in-law, and his grandson were able to make good their escape. All four returned to Europe. In Venice, the son-in-law Tupaka Umaru was murdered by hired killers.

Sebastian and Umira were in no doubt at all that the Spaniards were hot on their trail, and they determined to take refuge at Niedzica. At least they would be safe surrounded by their vassals in this distant province, much of which belonged to Benesh family. But they were wrong, for the henchmen of the Spaniards somehow slipped into the castle and stabbed Umira to death in the very courtyard where we were now standing, at the door of the new chapel. Sebastian himself barely had time to bury his daughter under the crypt before he had to leave—in a hurry.

Sebastian then retired to a monastery in

Kraków, where he died. In the meantime he sent his grandson to Krumlak, in Moravia, where the long arm of his Spanish enemy could not reach him. Umira had brought with her to Niedzica three huge chests which she had had buried somewhere in the mountains by her Indian slaves, who were sworn to secrecy. Her servants also noticed that Umira never allowed herself to be separated from a certain object, a cylindrical box about four inches long, which she appeared to value very highly. This box was not found on her body after the murder, and the Spanish agents responsible for her death disappeared without finding either this box or the three chests.

The grandson of Sebastian Benesh grew up in the safety and anonymity of a monastery in Moravia. Eventually he married a Polish girl and joined the army of Napoleon, where he had a brilliant career and won an enviable reputation for courage. He never claimed the dangerous inheritance of his grandfather, nor returned to Niedzica; instead he founded his own dynasty and the Benesh family continued tranquilly from generation to generation until the Second World War. At the end of this conflict, the last descendant of Sebastian Benesh called his only son, Andrei, to his deathbed and revealed the secret which he had carried with him throughout his life. Behind the altar of the Church of the Holy Cross at Kraków he had hidden a vital document concerning the Benesh ancestors.

No sooner was his father in the grave than Andrei hurried to the priest at the Church of the Holy Cross, who happened also to be a distant relative: and together they found the hiding place and drew out an old parchment. Andrei read this with feverish interest. It seemed that his ancestress, the Inca princess, had not only brought home to Niedzica a priceless hoard of gold; she had also known the whereabouts of the fabled treasure of the Incas, eagerly sought but never found since the conquest of America. This secret was (of course) contained in the cylindrical box which had never left her person.

Andrei's first move was to find out what had happened to Niedzica since his family's departure. The castle had reverted to Poland when that country regained its independence at the end of the First World War, while remaining firmly in the hands of its Hungarian owners, the Salomon family, who had succeeded the Beneshes. The advent of the Communist regime had finally dispossessed the Salomons, and the castle had been empty and abandoned ever since. God knows what arguments Andrei Benesh used with the archaeological service, but the fact remains that when he arrived at Niedzica

one fine day in 1946, accompanied by his wife and several hangers-on, he was able to flourish an official authorization to excavate in, and around, the castle. For this enterprise he recruited peasants and local policemen— as well as the young warden of the castle, Franciszek Szydlak, then only nineteen.

Franciszek himself told us what happened next. He has now reached a more respectable age and his flamboyant mustaches are frosted with white, but he still wears the red Hungarian livery with silver frogging left over from his teens, when Niedzica was still the private property of the Salomon family.

The arrival of Andrei Benesh completely upset the monotony of his existence and he watched this interesting rogue with growing interest. Andrei marched his little group of treasure hunters to the gateway leading into the oldest part of the castle. The stone of the threshold was an immense monolith which, with much cursing and grunting and shoving, they managed to lever up. Underneath was a small cylindrical box about four inches long. Andrei opened this and poured out its contents before the fascinated witnesses.

First came a handful of yellowish dust. Some of the people present concluded that this must be gold dust, but Franciszek recognized it as a very unusual sand, found on the banks of the River Vistula, far away from Niedzica.

After this another object slipped into the palm of Andrei's hand, a small stick from which hung twelve knotted cords. Andrei, who appeared well informed about this object, called it a *kipu*; he explained that the positioning of the knots on the tiny cords represented a secret code invented by the Incas. Franciszek, quietly looking on, observed that three of the twelve strings bore tiny golden heads engraved with esoteric markings which, according to Andrei Benesh, indicated in each case a holy site where the treasure of the Incas had been hidden after it was divided up. He claimed that these three sites were Lake Titicaca, the River Dunajac which ran along at the foot of the castle, and Lake Vigo. He was clearly wrong about this last site because there is no lake in existence called Vigo. On the other hand, it is know that a gigantic treasure from Peru sank, along with the ship transporting it, to the bottom of the Bay of Vigo in northern Spain, during the eighteenth century; and of this only a tiny proportion was recovered in the 1930s.

After his discovery of the *kipu*, Andrei left Niedzica, only to pop up again unexpectedly a couple of years later in company with a foreign professor. This time he stayed around for several weeks, methodically searching the interior of the castle as well as the surrounding land. Then he went away again.

Fifteen years elapsed, in which time Andrei Benesh became a powerful figure in the Communist Party, with considerable money and resources at his disposal. News reached Franciszek that Andrei was trying to mount some kind of an expedition to Peru and had recruited professional divers equipped with everything necessary for extensive underwater excavations. But on the eve of his departure, he was killed in a car accident. At this point Franciszek made it clear to us that Andrei's father, when he revealed the secret, had strongly advised his son to stay well away from it: there was, he said, something evil and incomprehensible about the whole business.

Well, of course I found this story so delightfully morbid and extravagant that I ached to believe it. Sergiusz, the curator of the castle, was the one who brought me down to earth. He pointed out that nobody had actually seen the original parchment found behind the altar of the Church of the Holy Cross. Benesh had only shown copies of this, and the experts who had examined the "original" document had found enough errors in it to make them suspect it was a fake. As for the *kipu* and the code in knotted string indicating where the treasure was, a large number of witnesses had seen this with their own eyes, even though it had subsequently disappeared. But these witnesses

were ordinary farming people and minor local functionaries, not experts, so Andrei Benesh could easily have made the thing himself and buried it under the threshold of the old castle the night before he "discovered" it.

"That's out of the question," objected old Franciszek. "I was there when they lifted the stone. I even helped them lift it, and I can assure you that nothing had been touched for centuries. And what about all those unexplained deaths?"

A few weeks after the *kipu*'s discovery, several of the peasants and policemen who had taken part in the investigation died suddenly. The curator didn't deny this: he even enriched the story with new details. A few years earlier, someone living in Katowice, claiming to be in touch with a clairvoyant, had written to ask for the plans of the castle—in which, according to him, there was plenty left to explore. The curator sent him a photocopy of the plans, but the clairvoyant was struck dead by a heart attack in the act of laying them out on his table. Then Sergiusz revealed that one of his predecessors, the castle's first curator, had drowned in the river. And the second curator never returned from a trip to Nepal—nobody ever heard what happened to him.

"Aren't you worried on your own behalf?" I asked naively.

I swear I saw his eyes flicker. Sergiusz was a refined, well-bred man, but his hair was prematurely gray. He smiled sadly.

"The fact that I'm still alive and kicking means I don't believe a word of all this."

He said this in such a way that I immediately suspected the contrary. He was visibly obsessed by the mystery of Niedzica.

We talked on and on about it over our meal in the castle's huge dining room. Outside, night was falling, and we were the only guests beneath the heavy painted beams. I made the remark that there must be some mention or other of the Inca princess. Sergiusz shook his head: no trace of her had ever been found.

"Well," I said, "that's the end of it. She never even existed!"

"Who knows? The archives were so badly handled during the Communist era that they haven't even been catalogued, let alone deciphered."

I asked about the various excavations at the castle, which were carried out with the utmost care, to no avail at all. "The princess's silver coffin doesn't exist. No coffin, no princess."

"Who can say?" said Sergiusz. "We've only been through a very small part of the castle."

I realized that the farther I advanced toward the Inca princess, the thicker the shadows surrounding her became. Her story was so outlandish that it could be neither entirely true, nor yet entirely invented. Sergiusz, deepening the atmosphere of mystery, suggested a nocturnal tour of the premises.

Niedzica, which had become an important venue for conferences and seminars, happened at that time to be full of academics. Several of these eagerly showed us their guest apartments, in which a few of them claimed to have been shoved to the bottoms of their beds in the small hours, very probably by the Inca princess. Old Franciszek then insisted that we open up the curator's offices. He told us he had been there several decades before with an engineer whose job was to check the castle's fittings. Suddenly a strong wind howled through the building, so violently that it flung open the steel doors. A ball of light appeared and approached the two men with fantastic speed. When it reached them, it took the form of a woman, scaring the two men almost out of their wits. That evening Franciszek told this story to his mother, who had once been the Salomons' chambermaid. She told him mildly that the same thing had happened on a number of occasions before the war and that it was nothing to get excited about.

As we wandered through the darkness from wing to wing of the castle, I found my attention drawn toward the huge blind keep which glowered over the rest of the fortress. Gradually, the conviction grew in my mind that if there was indeed something here, it was behind those massive walls.

Eventually we came to the threshold of the old castle beneath which Andrei Benesh had discovered the buried *kipu*. After exploring the oubliettes (which I was quite certain had never been used for any nefarious purpose) we came to a torture chamber filled with luridly fascinating instruments. Then we climbed into a more recent building backing on to the keep. The first room here, which was whitewashed, empty of furniture, and without atmosphere, opened onto a second space containing a collection of ordinary family clocks. This decor could hardly have been more familiar and soothing, but I felt a growing discomfort.

The third room in the suite was within the wall of the donjon, which could be penetrated here by way of the second floor. It was a continuation of the museum, and in it a peasant's cottage had been reconstructed complete with wooden walls, low roof, windows, furniture, and everyday objects. But however charming and intimate the decor, I found that this room sent shivers up my spine. It exuded a repulsive and very strong impression of blood and violence.

What was in the room above? Attics. We climbed into these by way of a narrow wooden staircase. Three rooms, one on top of the other, each occupied one floor of the donjon. All of them were stacked with dust-covered bric-a-brac. These three rooms were also haunted, but less powerfully and nastily than the fake peasant's cottage on the first floor. I therefore installed myself alone in the attic, right above it.

With some difficulty I managed to open a worm-eaten door which had obviously been closed for many centuries. It gave on to what once had been a balcony.

The moon outside was approaching the full. Far below me I could see the landscape of darkened rivers, meadows, and hills, glimmering peacefully under the night sky. I sat myself down to wait on the lid of a humpbacked trunk . . . My eye ran along the shelves, which were stacked with pottery, straw dolls, and, for some obscure reason, souvenirs of the First World War. Despite all these cozy objects, the same ugly waves of violence and bloodshed kept flowing over me. Yet I wasn't afraid, because I felt somehow that I was welcome. There was someone in the room with me, a woman. She was no Inca princess. What I felt was something far older. No: she emanated from the Middle Ages.

· · ·

I belonged to a very great and ancient family, and this castle was only one of our many properties.

Ours was a pitiless stock. Savage and fearless as we were, the sight of the most hideous sufferings had no power to move us. Nevertheless I lived out my early years in far more civilized surroundings than this fortress: in palaces, in great cities, and in castles in the richest, most populated regions of our country.

As a little girl, I loved to hide behind walls and curtains to observe what was forbidden for me to see. In this way I learnt everything there was to know about desire, perversion, and excess, before I was old enough to begin indulging in these things myself. And my taste for cruelty showed early. I inflicted pain on my playmates and discovered that this produced both attraction and repulsion. The little girls detested me. Some of the boys stayed out of my way, but others allowed themselves to be entrapped.

My father saw his own nature mirrored in mine and he dared not treat me harshly, so awed was he by the fact that his most secret and shameful personality had been passed on to me. Nevertheless my parents did their best to teach me discipline, even though they were obliged to admit defeat after a very short time. In the end I was simply allowed to grow up willy-nilly. Nobody gave much thought to what would become of me.

When I reached my teens, an attempt was made to arrange a marriage with a great lord whose fortune and rank were equal to mine.

Inconceivable though this may seem, given the time in which I lived, I flatly refused. The way I saw it, this union meant little more than a lifetime of imprisonment. Although until that time nobody had dared to do such a thing, I faced down not only my father and my mother, but also all the other men in my family. Nobody dared confront me, and certainly nobody dared to punish me.

I always loved Niedzica. I found its isolation strangely attractive. Seeing this, my family was only too happy to hand the place over to me; it amounted to sending me away to the most distant place they could think of. When I settled here I understood I had been brought to Niedzica by some mysterious force, for in this castle my primitive instincts were unleashed at last.

In one wing of the castle were the apartments normally reserved for the nobles of my family. I preferred to set up my headquarters in the keep, which at that time was nothing more than a defensive fortification. I converted it to suit my own tastes, painting the ceilings and the beams, hanging tapestries on the walls, and covering the creaking floorboards with precious rugs and carpets.

How many times have I stood on this little balcony, staring out at the landscape! All I could see then was a village with a few tumbledown hovels, then miles of forests and plain. There were no roads. I wanted the wild landscape to stay the same forever.

Every day, I mounted my horse and set off on wild gallops among the hills and woods. I knew there were bands of vicious brigands who would certainly lie in wait for me. This certainty thrilled me. I crammed my spurs into my horse's bleeding flanks and several times arrived home only to feel the poor brute die under me in the courtyard. All I wanted from my mounts was that they should carry me away like the wind. If they could not do this, they were useless to me. Yet, in my way, I loved all creatures, and when I killed them in the hunt, I did so to eat and to give to eat.

Men in my eyes were no more than another way to calm my ardor. When a man attracted me, I brought him to my bed. None stayed for long. I didn't hold this against them. I knew there would be plenty of others.

It was not arrogance which led me to excess but my own nature. My only duty in life was to obey that nature, and never resist it because it was always right. I was intoxicated with my freedom, with the wide spaces at my disposal, and with all extremes. For me, freedom and extremity were one. My rule was never to flinch in the face of danger, and believe me, everything around me reeked of danger.

When war broke out in our province and enemy forces approached, it was I who organized the defense of Niedzica. I watched their hordes come marching down the river, round the fortress which guards its further bank. Methodically they laid siege to Niedzica and for many weeks we resisted; but finally the castle fell. At the last moment, I escaped through a secret passage, which still exists today. Our enemies had overrun the courtyards and the keep and the only soldiers left on our side had barricaded themselves into the highest room of the building. Finally they were overwhelmed by sheer weight of numbers and cut to pieces. Their blood soaked these walls. Shortly afterwards, our king sent in an army to retake the castle and when I returned again, it was to find my apartments smeared with purple stains.

Killing was my particular pleasure. I never carried out physical torture with my own hands, but I liked to have others do so and observe my victims—who were usually petty criminals—in their agony.

I longed to know by what secret mechanism life is tipped at last into the abyss of death—or of eternity. I wanted to watch the approach of that moment: I meant to decipher the mystery of it. I groped for the farthest reaches of knowledge, power, and cruelty. In doing this, I also put myself through a fearsome ordeal. I could not bear the sight of blood. Ever since my childhood, blood had made me sick to my stomach, and in consequence I decided to live in blood so that I could overcome this fear. I never did anything by half measures, which to me meant mediocrity.

All my life I committed horror after horror. Crime was my companion and the blood I shed was my comfort. And now that I am a ghost, I feel the need to tell of it, to escape the solitude in which my secret has cloistered me.

Then the danger I had courted all my life began to close in. The peasants whispered about my doings and eventually one of them repeated the rumors at a market in town. The news spread quickly to the capital of the province, and from there rushed on to the capital of the realm. An inquiry was ordered, and one day some knights appeared at Niedzica under the royal banner. With them was a judge exhausted by the tedious journey, furious that he had been delegated for this mission, and already strongly biased against me.

I was obliged to receive him. But nothing would make me abase myself so far as to answer the questions of that churl, even if he did represent the king's justice, and I refused to appear before him. I therefore left Niedzica and went to a castle which my family owned not far away. Without so much as a by-your-leave, the judge installed himself in my private apartments, and here he summoned my servants to testify against me.

He did not know that I was watching him. I came back to the castle secretly. I had the gift of moving about unseen, like a cat, and I would slip into the smallest hiding place to observe and listen as the questions were asked and answered. Although my serfs stoutly refused to denounce their mistress, he managed to trick them into saying what they had sworn they would never say. The case against me grew stronger and in the papers piled on his table, I read my doom. I could have

had him killed on the spot, or cut down in the forest along with the royal guards. Suspicion might have fallen on me, but nobody would have dared pursue the investigation any further. Instead I did nothing. To let nature speak is to let fate run its course. I accepted that my fate should be decided before my eyes.

I went back to Niedzica, where I was immediately arrested. I could have called my people to release me, but even then I did nothing. The judge had me imprisoned on the first floor of the keep, in the room which is now used as a museum of arts and crafts.

On his own authority, he instituted a tribunal. It was his wish that I be tried in my own castle with all the trappings of royal justice, and he held his court in my favorite room, this one, which opens onto the balcony.

The witnesses, who were the principal employees of the castle and the estate, constituted the vox populi: this was an important element in the system of justice at that time, and it was organized as an official legal body. When I appeared before my judge, surrounded by his guards, I suddenly woke from my trance. I spat upon him, crying that he had no right to sit in judgment here. At this he drew the royal mandate from his sleeve and justified his perversion of justice by the isolation of the place and the need to put an immediate end to my crimes.

Then he read out the evidence against me. It was overwhelming. I sensed behind me the silent presence of the men and women who knew everything there was to know about me. For many years they had served me loyally without fear or favor, and I believed that my rule had been a fair one, despite my cruelties. For the first time, however, I realized that they were judging me.

I stood in front of the table at which the judge was sitting and I watched him as he read out the sentence of death. Then he asked all those present for their approval. Silence. Then I turned around and looked at them. They lowered their eyes and the judge wrote on his parchment that the vox populi approved my sentence.

If I were thrown into prison for any length of time, my family, even though it was well aware of my crimes, would certainly intercede with the king to obtain a pardon; and if I were led out to be executed publicly, the people might riot and release me. The judge therefore decreed that I be executed immediately, in the room which had earlier served as my prison.

I was forced to kneel. Because there was no block, I was made to lay my head sideways on the lid of a chest. My hair was pulled up, and my neck bared. There was no bandage for my eyes. The soldier who had been chosen as my executioner was without experience. There was no axe, either, so he made do with a halberd; halberds are designed to be used like scythes, not like cutting swords.

Not surprisingly, my executioner clean missed with his first blow and thereafter struck several times, slicing deep into my arm, face, and shoulder before finally hitting my neck. The pain was atrocious, but I would not die. At last the other guards came to finish me with their daggers. They were hardened veterans and although some were drunk with the bloodletting, other were ready to vomit. I had insisted before my death that my execution should be made known down to the last detail, partly as a vengeance on those who killed me and partly so that the horror of my death should efface the horror of my crimes. I, who had caused so much blood to flow, would atone for it with my own.

The judge never recovered from the spectacle of my death, and died a stricken man. In the archives and chronicles, there is almost no mention of me; my family convinced the king that the trial should go unrecorded. Thus I retained my noble status and no shame rubbed off on my relatives. Niedzica, which had never by right belonged to me, reverted to the family.

Several centuries later, there was a Sebastian Benesh here who went away to seek his fortune in Peru. He can't have been very successful because he remained obscure. One of his daughters lived at Niedzica, and because of her father's association with South America, where she was born, she was nicknamed the Inca princess. She had nothing whatever to do with the castle treasure, which really does exist; though it is something far older than either she or I. It includes gold and gems, but its value goes far beyond these. It has magical properties of enormous potency, derived from a branch of Freemasonry that existed here in the early years of Christianity. When the treasure ceased to be of use, it was buried, its substance being too dangerous to destroy. Traces of this secret came down to the twentieth century, and inspired people like Andrei Benesh to come here in search of it.

This last Benesh came across a document referring to it in the Church of the Holy Cross at Kraków. He then researched the castle's history, found a distant ancestor called the "Inca princess," and constructed the fiction of a descendant of the Grand Inca who came to die in rural Poland. The entire story was designed to throw other treasure hunters off the scent: the kipu was real enough, having been brought here with a number of other trinkets by the "Inca princess," but it had absolutely no connection with the treasure.

I have to say that I too was involved in this arcane treasure hunt. One day a man came to Niedzica, wanting permission to search the castle. He wouldn't tell me why, so I put him to the torture. I found out that the secret could only be unraveled if you solved a certain enigma, which my man knew of but had as yet failed to penetrate. I determined to take up the problem where he had left off, more from a determination not to be thwarted than from any greed for gold. Curiously enough, the same motives seem to have swayed all the other seekers who came here over the centuries.

To decipher the code a particular form of intelligence was required, one close to madness . . .

Moreover, the treasure itself was tainted by the power of black magic, in that black magic was the only means by which it could be found. And consequently those who embarked on the search ran the risk of unleashing destructive forces on themselves. When I tackled the enigma, I paid for it very dearly; and so did Andrei Benesh centuries later. Many others have gone the same way, and if I do not say more it is to protect my listeners.

May this castle go down to utter ruin before the secret is revealed; the treasure of Niedzica is best left well alone.

A SECRET SCANDAL

Zaraus, Spain

THE CLIMATE HERE IS WET BUT healthy, temperate and agreeable. . . . rheumatism, haemorroids, colds and certain heart disorders are practically the only chronic ailments observed. The latter are much influenced in their proliferation by the hard labour which occupies the majority of the population. Nevertheless many local people reach the advanced ages of ninety and even a hundred years old."

This interesting description, culled from a mid-nineteenth-century geographical dictionary, lent a certain attraction to the area of the Basque country to which we had come. Nevertheless, when the little resort of Zaraus was revealed to us around a bend in the road, it gave little promise, in my eyes, of supernatural occupation. Of course ghosts can lurk just about anywhere, but I was worried that even they might be taken aback by these rows of bland seaside constructions and hideous modern villas.

Yet somewhere in this mess the palace of Narros lay concealed.

"It's on the right, the last house in the village. Ask anyone, they'll direct you straight to it."

I had expected a ponderous art deco villa at best, so what were my surprise and

delight when Justin and I found ourselves confronted with a walled garden planted with tall, straight trees, enclosing a building which seemed half fortress, half manor house. The heavily emblazoned ocher facade was pure seventeenth century.

We rang at the heavy, studded door, and Doña Feli Odriofola herself immediately opened it, as if her hand had been resting on the latch. This generously proportioned person fairly exuded authority, and the delicate courtesy with which she received us did nothing to disguise the underlying force of her character. She immediately launched into a flood of reminiscence. From this I gleaned the central fact that she had been the guardian of the old house for twenty-eight years—and in all important respects the mistress of it, given the virtually permanent absence of the owners. The illustrious name of the family she had served so loyally filled her with pride; and with good reason, for the dukes of Villahermosa belong to one of the most ancient and revered houses in Spain. Their history is a long accumulation of feats of arms, royal dynasties, famous men, castles, collections, and titles.

Doña Feli proudly conducted us past the portraits of Villahermosa ancestors gathered on the walls. Here was the Marquis de Narros, wearing in his picture the selfsame apricot-colored silk cloth which Doña Feli now extracted from a beautifully worked chest, for us to finger. And here was the Contessa de Bureta, in peasant costume, brandishing her heavy blunderbuss, a heroine of the war of resistance against Napoleon's invading armies. Alas, on the walls of several salons the frames hung blind and empty, their contents having been neatly removed by thieves.

Next we were shown through the covered patio, bright with potted flowers and bougainvilleas, to a series of old-fashioned salons giving on to a magnificent view. At our feet extended the beach and the jade-green ocean. It happened to be the anniversary of the local sporting club, and fifty-two amateur football teams were playing twenty-six simultaneous football matches on the sand, to the unbridled admiration of the populace. The noise produced by this crowd was guaranteed to send any ghost in its right mind scudding for cover.

All the same, the basement to which Doña Feli now led us was most intriguing. It seemed altogether too subtly planned and elegantly built to have been meant as cellar space alone. Perhaps, I thought, we were standing on the first floor of a much older building. As my nineteenth-century chronicler had wearily pointed out, the origins of this were "lost in the mists of time."

"Before there was Zaraus, there was only

Zaraus," says the gnomic village motto. On the other hand, the Palacio Narros, which was the seat of an entailed property from the early Middle Ages and the center of an immense estate, was considered to be the oldest noble house in the province. Its owners unswervingly served the crown, and it was therefore heavily involved with wars against first the Moors, then against the English and the French. In the nineteenth century it was briefly a royal palace when Isabella II made it her summer residence; indeed it was while she was here that the queen was obliged (much to her irritation) to recognize the new Kingdom of Italy. On that occasion she received the smooth ambassador of the Savoys in a salon on the second floor. This ambassador was the Duke of Aosta, who a few years later was to replace Isabella herself on the Spanish throne, following a bewildering series of revolutions and coups d'état. The vermeil filigreed inkpot she used to sign the official recognition is still in place.

Next we visited the garden side of the house. In the second-floor salon containing the portraits of the ducal family's contingent of saints, several effigies of Ignatius de Loyola were ponderously present, to remind us that he was one of the most illustrious Villahermosa ancestors. After this came a bedroom hung with blue fabric, more aus-

terely furnished than the rest. "This is where *El Dracula* appeared," spat Doña Feli, who clearly had no liking for this figure.

With a certain judicious pumping up of the imagination I expect I could have believed that corpses were packed like anchovies into the wardrobes, but I sincerely doubted that any vampire would have dared to confront the formidable Doña Feli. Yet the latter was a trifle reticent about him. Luckily her pretty daughter Mirem, who now joined us, was much more willing than her mother to talk about the resident phantoms.

Long ago, she said, there was a storm at sea and a ship was driven ashore at Zaraus. Only one man from the crew managed to swim ashore. The family took him into the palace and sheltered him in this room, called the Blue Room. But before long the local people began to murmur against the newcomer, a Protestant heretic who had fled the civil war then raging in France. Many claimed that he wasn't even a Christian. In any event, it was voted highly undesirable that he should remain at Zaraus. The stranger protested that he was a good Catholic, but to no avail: the suspicions of the villagers grew and grew, until the moment when the man suddenly fell ill.

He retired to the huge ornate bed of blackwood I was now contemplating and before long was writhing in agony. The priest was called to give him the last rites, but on the brink of death, he could no longer keep up the lie he had been living, and vomited forth his bile and hatred of the true religion. As he did so, a tongue of flame spurted from the wall and leapt from one end of the palace to the other.

The man was dead, but now the question arose, where should he be buried? "Certainly not in our cemetery," howled the villagers. So the family disposed of the corpse in secret, nobody knew where. Some said he was stuffed beneath the stone cross which formerly stood in the garden, others that he was immured in the wall of the bedroom, and still others that he had been tossed back into the sea from whence he had come.

Nobody had much cared for the nameless heretic while he lived, and now that he was dead they liked him even less, particularly when he started to haunt the Palacio de Narros in a variety of unpleasant ways. His legend, regularly embroidered with fresh beastlinesses, came down through the centuries to our own, at which time crazy Father Coloma came to investigate the case *in situ.*

This holy man demanded to spend the night in the Blue Room. Just after the stroke of midnight, Father Coloma was still awake and deep in contemplation when a burning sphere fell from the ceiling of the salon adjoining, whose door was wide open: this sphere then bounced into the haunted room, skittered up to the priest's feet, burned a quick hole in the floor, and through it plummeted into the room below. It left behind it a noisome odor of scorching, which lingers in the Blue Room still.

Father Coloma immediately made a literary name for himself with his romantic account of this experience, entitled *The Blue Chamber.*

Later, another priest, the exorcist Father Pilon, arrived with all the sophisticated paraphernalia of a professional ghost-hunter and made a series of recordings in the haunted room. When these were played over, they produced an incomprehensible gabble overlaid by the shrill sound of a woman's voice, with a general effect not unlike Spanish radio.

The ducal family all agreed that the voice was that of "Tante Germaine," a French governess who had succeeded in marrying the Marquis de Narros. Germaine was a good-looker and an artist, a member of the Resistance who had won high honors for her courage, but her noble in-laws nonetheless suspected her of *arrivisme* and kept her relentlessly at arm's length.

The years went by, and the agitations of

Father Pilon and "the Frenchwoman" were forgotten. Then, in the mid-1980s, the three grandchildren of the Duquesa de Villahermosa (they were triplets, two boys and a girl, aged seven) came to spend the summer holidays at the Palacio de Narros. On several occasions they told their governess and their parents that they had seen a tall, pretty lady in a long dress walking in the gallery surrounding the patio. Not much notice was taken. The children had read too many horror stories or goggled at too much television. Whereupon a small cousin of the same age declared that she too had glimpsed the lady. Perhaps, after all, the Frenchwoman was coming back to Narros to torture the family that had spurned her. Pressed to describe what she had seen, the child gave a brisk account that did not sound in any respect like "Tante Germaine"; and anyway the Narros ghost was supposed to be a man, to wit the shipwrecked Huguenot. So public opinion turned against the little cousin, who was assumed to have invented the whole thing.

For my own part, I greatly preferred Queen Isabella's room to the "Dracula Bedroom." Plenty of money had been spent on it in anticipation of the royal visit, and it was probably in the queen's honor that a magnificent suite of furniture had been wheeled in. All of it was in the purest nineteenth-century Baroque style, in dark wood encrusted with pearly coral. The room was made even more enticing by sumptuous flowered wallpaper, and even the roar and rasp of the ocean—which in the interval had completely covered the beach, driving the footballers like foam before it—could not detract from its atmosphere of jolliness and serenity. There was no question in my mind that the house was haunted through and through, but its welcome to us was nonetheless warm and cordial for that. In fact it surrounded me, cherished me, and begged me to stay awhile.

I felt a special ambience of welcome in the bedroom of Queen Isabella.

The pale winter sun outside was not enough to justify the sheer warmth of that room. Here was warmth of another kind, I was sure, a human warmth which caressed and enveloped me. There was even a perfume of love in the air. I thought of Queen Isabella, whose volcanic affairs had been the talk of Spain. Yet the woman who insinuated herself into my consciousness was another person altogether, a tall, slender creature. I knew that she was a beauty, though I was unable to make out her features. She wore gold-embroidered velvet from head to foot; heavy jewels and a broad ruff framed her face. To judge by her clothes, she must have belonged to the court of one of the Philips.

But what on earth was she doing dressed up in full regalia, way out here in the country?

In the earliest times, a sage lived here. He came from a far country, and had walked far, guided by a star that brought him to this place. Enchanted by its beauty and tranquillity, he made it his home, building a rough hermitage and spreading blessings around him. Before long his fame attracted disciples, who succeeded him after his death. These built a small monastery around the well which is now to be found in the palace cellars. In their primitive quarters, the monks concocted remedies with medicinal herbs, fruits, and vegetables. They did not sell these, but exchanged them for food with the peasants of the region.

Later the monks died out and their priory fell into ruin. For many centuries the site was abandoned, but he pious village people kept alive the memory of the monks and cherished the site's reputation for beneficence.

Then the ancestors of the present owners came, acquiring the conviction that in this place a treasure was concealed; not understanding that it was a treasure of the soul only, and not some mine of precious metal. They made use of the foundation built by the monks to create the cellars of the present palace. They expected to unearth marvels, but there was only the ocean and the moaning of the wind, and they cursed the villagers for deceiving them.

But the castle was now in place, and so had to be visited from time to time, especially since the family had acquired other lands in the vicinity. Over the years, a steady procession of grandees came here, some of whom divined the simple essence of Zaraus, and some of whom did not. Yet it was a curious fact that they were all fond of this place, to which their forebears had been attracted by a simple error of interpretation.

Then came the famous shipwreck. The hapless victim was not a Protestant but a Muslim corsair, of the ruthless breed which infested the seas at that time. He was inordinately strong, and it was this strength alone which saved his life when his companions perished. Like the original hermit, the corsair never paused to wonder why he had come here, but as soon as he came ashore instinctively set about destroying the peace he discovered around him. In this he did not reckon with the power which, though it revitalizes the creature of good, burns the man of evil to his very entrails. The pirate failed in his destructive endeavor, and was himself destroyed. He was hurled back into the sea from which he had come.

About a hundred years after these events, I became the owner of the palace. I was a great lady, the holder of a high rank at court. My husband was grave and hard working, colorless perhaps,

but generous and charitable for a man in his position. I cherished him and our children, I loved my life, and I loved the many different castles and manor houses we visited so regularly on our tours of inspection.

From the earliest years of our marriage I was attracted to this house, even though in my time coming here was like coming to the end of the world. Our visit were rare. When we traveled, we were accompanied by large numbers of servants, along with a small court of our own, which filled the house to bursting. Whenever I could, I went away by myself. I cast off my farthingales, my starched ruffs, and my embroidered velvet gowns, and I ran down to the orchard to pick fruit or into the fields to wander in the growing wheat.

One day I was walking on a rough track, thinking of nothing in particular. A gentle breeze was blowing and the clouds scudded in the sky. I was carefree and light-footed beside the fruit trees and the flowering bushes. A man came walking toward me. As we passed each other, our eyes met, and in that instant I was lost.

Nothing in our separate lives could have brought us together under normal circumstances, yet that one chance glimpse was enough to set us both ablaze. It was the kind of love which could transcend life; yet it led straight to disaster.

The following day I returned to the same place at the same hour, quite certain he would be there waiting for me. And so he was. I spoke to him

briefly. He told me he had come in search of work and had been hired in our absence. Thereafter I went back almost every day. The things we said to each other were entirely proper, but our eyes spoke of other things.

One evening, I stayed late with him, then suddenly realized that I would have to hurry back to the house if I was to arrive before dark. He grasped my hand to keep me and suddenly I was in his arms. We made love immediately, on the bare ground, under the trees.

Soon I returned to Madrid with my family, living only for the day of my return. Little by little I arranged for our stays at Narros to last longer. My husband was happy to agree.

Eventually my separations from my lover became intolerable. We couldn't have enough of each other.

Here in the house I wrote to him each day before I saw him and each night when I returned from our trysts. My love letters covered page after page, and I passed them on to him. In return he brought me flowers, and sometimes the gift of a bauble picked up at the village market, a shred of lace or some silk.

Then he gave me some silver earrings, which seemed to me far more precious than the family heirlooms with which my husband had loaded me on the day of our wedding, the monstrous diamonds of which he was so proud. I had to wear the earrings when I was alone in my apartments, or *when I met my lover, for fear that they would arouse the suspicions of those around me.*

Then came the day that I stayed too late in his arms and in my haste forgot to remove the earrings. My family immediately noticed them and inquired where they came from. I said they were peasant things I had found, which I thought suited me: they might even launch a fashion at court . . . This seemed to satisfy them.

In reality from the day my lover entered my life I had changed profoundly, and so had my family. I became indifferent to my children, and a gulf suddenly yawned between my husband and myself.

The next winter, when I was in Madrid, I begged to be allowed to return to Zaraus, even in this most unseasonable time. I claimed that I needed spiritual repose, which surprised my husband, who knew I was no zealot. And I knew immediately that he suspected me, to such an extent that I considered giving up the plan. But it was too late. I had already imagined how it would be when I flew into my lover's arms, and I lacked the strength to deny myself that bliss.

My husband agreed to let me go—on condition that I take a priest with me to guide my contemplation. He would not part with the chaplain who officiated each day at our palace in Madrid, but he undertook to find another who was free to come to Zaraus.

A priest was found and we set off on the long, hard journey northward. The rain fell incessant-

ly, so that the roads became close to impassable. The horses could only manage a few miles each day in the mud and cold, and my tiny retinue complained bitterly: only the priest spoke not a word. He knew already that I was not pious, since I resolutely declined his invitations to say the rosary. On the other hand this journey, which for the others was a dismal nightmare, was to me like a promenade through an enchanted garden. The cold, the rain, the wind, and the discomfort were nothing to me.

We arrived at Narros in the evening, at the supper hour, when everything was already plunged in darkness. I hoped that my lover might have got wind of my coming because of the fuss it had caused, and I possessed myself in patience until the meal was over. The priest sat in silence, slowly chewing his food and staring at me covertly.

At last I was able to take my leave. I put on a heavy veil, slipped out of the house, and ran to our favorite trysting place, hoping my lover would be there. He was waiting. All that night the icy rain fell and the wind moaned, yet it felt as if the sun was shining steadily on us where we lay together. Just before daybreak I reentered the house, as easily as I had left it.

I had to indulge the priest, however, and to this end I asked him for help with my rosary. But whenever I closed my eyes to recite the Aves the image of my lover rose before me. Day after day the priest droned on about the sacred texts, while I struggled to remain awake after my nights of love. He watched me secretly, but I was so happy I couldn't care less. I was fool enough to think his condition as a man of God absolved me from the precautions I should otherwise have taken.

At last I was caught—by one of the chambermaids, who saw me leaving the house in a simple dress and shawl. I stuttered something about fresh air, but went back upstairs like a guilty child; then I waited a couple of hours before creeping forth again, this time encountering no one. My lover was there to meet me and I fell into his arms: it was our last night, and everyone else was desperately eager to return to Madrid. We would be parted until the coming of spring, but the time we had spent together had given me such joy that I was ready for the ordeal. When we said goodbye, I was light of heart.

My return to Madrid was more easily accomplished than my coming, bathed as I was in the afterglow of love. But the day after my arrival my husband summoned me to his cavernous office. Without a word, he handed me a sheaf of letters I had written to my lover. Throughout our stay at Zaraus, the priest had spied upon me. He had caused my lover's belongings to be searched, and from my letters had selected a few of the most ardent to show my husband.

Without a word I made my way back to my apartments. For three days and nights I was allowed to cool my heels alone; nobody came to me but the chambermaids, who slipped in and out as quietly as possible, in dread of the scene that was

bound to come. Meantime I sank into despair.

On the fourth day, my husband told me a place had been found in a convent that his family had patronized for many centuries. This meant he was condemning me to life imprisonment. I knew it was useless to object: nobody would help me, indeed nobody would be especially surprised at my withdrawal from the scene. I had not been noted for my deep faith, but the pure of heart would certainly be persuaded that God had called me, and that I had responded to the call. It would look as if the deed had been done of my own free will.

I asked to be spared the pain of a farewell to my children.

I left the palace that very night, after a last lonely tour of the great reception rooms, the galleries, and the dimly lit staircases, all the time knowing well that an army of servants was waiting and spying on my every motion. Then I went to the carriage, which as usual was escorted by armed outriders. Only this time they were not protecting, but guarding me.

All night we traveled, reaching our destination at the crack of dawn. Before me loomed a high wall, pierced by a few heavily barred window embrasures. At the gates, all the inmates of the convent were turned out to welcome the devout wife of their benefactor.

I turned back once to view the countryside. The sky was turning from gray to pink, and the bare hilltops and rocky gullies lay sunk in bluish mist. On the horizon gleamed the first yellow rays of

sunshine. I shivered for cold, though the light gave promise of a fine hot day. Then I stepped across the threshold of the convent and the iron-banded gates clanged shut behind me.

I never took the veil. Like many men and women of my rank, who renounced the world but refused holy orders, I lived the monastic life, though with a greater measure of freedom than the nuns around me. I did not wear the cassock, contenting myself with the modest dress suitable for one in my case.

The name and the image of my lover were with me night and day; but there was no hope at all of further contact between us. I never knew what became of him.

Inside, I was cold ashes, and on the outside I slowly shriveled. I grew thin, and my skin turned to parchment. I did not bend or break, but my heart had burned so hotly that it was utterly consumed. I lived on, without the least desire to do so. So drained was I by the end that I lost even my yearning for my lover. It was several years before death came to me.

I do not haunt the convent, where I died, but this palace of Narros, where my greatest happiness and my ill fortune both befell me. I am like a kite, invisible in the clouds, shaking and shuddering at the whim of the breeze: and the living may only see me in function of the string that attaches me to the earth. I am everywhere and nowhere, so you see no more than an impression of my being. One day the string will be cut and the kite will float free. In the meantime, I am happy to be in this house, which is built on a blessed site. Narros is a place that breathes goodness, and those who come here are invigorated by that goodness and fall under its charm.

I am very discreet, but I could not resist showing myself to Queen Isabella when she slept in my room. When she woke and saw me, she abused me roundly for disturbing her. She meant to sleep and she didn't give a fig for ghosts, which pleased me well.

I so loved this house in my time that I would never dream of making a nuisance of myself in it. Pray for my lover, not for me. Where is he? Was he condemned to haunt the earth like I was, or did he go into the light when he died? I can't be sure. I only know that one day I shall see him again.

THE MISUNDERSTOOD CZAR

Palace of Pavlovsk, Russia

PAVLOVSK IS NEITHER THE LARGEST nor the most lavish of the Russian palaces, but it is beyond doubt the most refined and seductive. In front, the sober yellow-and-white facade arcs around a broad courtyard; behind, the building overlooks a lush valley and a meandering river. This countrified exterior gives no inkling of the opulence and delicacy of what lies within.

The greatest craftsmen of the late eighteenth century came to Pavlovsk with wood, bronze, ivory, marble, glass, and silk to create a masterpiece of incomparable taste; and despite the variety of elements and shapes it contains, the furniture, the chandeliers, the flooring, the bibelots, the hangings, and the chimneypieces form a magical, harmonious ensemble. Here decoration has risen to the level of great art, and I know of no decor whose beauty or quality comes near it. All around the palace extends a broad grass park, planted with woodlands and fed by lakes, all of which seem right and natural, but which are in fact the triumphant achievement of the greatest landscape architects of the period. It is good to walk here in any season.

Pavlovsk is dear to my heart because it belonged to my Russian great-grandfather, and it was the birthplace of my own father. He was christened in the white-and-gold chapel that I visited on the day the collapse of communism returned it to the church, after seventy years of atheist neglect.

Every year before the Revolution my father left Greece and traveled to Pavlovsk for a spell with his grandparents. Love of the palace was in his blood, and in spite of his youth he was astonished anew each time he came by the treasures of art it contained. At the same time he made a full and thorough inventory of the ghosts in the house, his special favorite being that which appeared to Grand Duchess Alexandra, his grandmother. I can still hear him telling the story:

"One evening, on her way to dinner, Alexandra was walking along the vaulted ground-floor gallery, in company with a couple of aides-de-camp. At a given moment, all three saw a woman in the distance walking down to meet them. The figure was dressed in white from head to foot, but there was otherwise nothing particularly unusual about her and they assumed she was a lady-in-waiting—until they realized that she was moving quite soundlessly. The setting sun cast sufficient light beneath the arches for them to see her quite clearly as she drew near.

"When the figure was within a few paces of my grandmother, she halted and stared straight into her eyes. Afterwards none of the three was able to recall the details of the face, and could only say that it was suffused with an expression of really shocking malice. My grandmother was seized with a horror so profound that she stopped dead in her tracks, unable to move: at which moment the creature surged forward as if to strike her.

"Seeing this, the two aides overcame their own paralysis and thrust themselves in the way. But their hands clutched at thin air: the figure had entirely vanished, as mysteriously as she had come.

"My grandmother was taken back to her apartments half-fainting with terror. Hearing the story, her women shuddered. "She has seen the White Lady," was the dire verdict, and my grandmother's anguish increased a hundredfold. Like all the other princesses, she was all too familiar with the story of the terrible wandering ghost which had haunted the family throughout history, wherever they happened to be, and whose manifestations invariably predicted a major catastrophe. Next day, sure enough, my grandmother's youngest son, Dmitri Constantinovitch, fell ill. Less than a week later, he was dead."

Then came the 1917 Revolution. Certain members of the imperial family contrived to escape abroad, while others—several of whom lived at Pavlovsk—were massacred.

My own grandmother Olga, because of her title of Queen Mother of Greece, remained in the palace largely undisturbed, quietly running the hospital for the war-wounded she had installed there. She shared with every other Russian the appalling privations of that time, living on bread and oil for over a year. Olga was the last of the family to reside at Pavlovsk.

One morning in spring, I returned to the palace for the fourth time in my life. The curator, Ludmila Koval, who always looks after me so kindly and efficiently, led me into one of the horseshoe-shaped wings, to the former apartments of my grandmother Olga, now used as a depot. In the course of my visit, I stumbled on a long black case made of tin. On the lid was written in white letters: "English Admiral's Uniform of His Imperial Majesty." I knew that Edward VII had offered this honorary distinction to his nephew Nicolas II, and I couldn't resist the temptation to open the trunk. But under the layers of paper I found not a uniform, but children's clothes made of white wool and edged with swans. These had belonged to the little grand duchesses and the czarevitch, who were later killed at Yekaterinenburg. The lady curators were just as moved and upset as I was, a proof that despite the Communist attempt to erase the memory of

that tragedy, it is still vividly present in the minds of ordinary Russians.

Later, in Queen Olga's salon, we sat around a broad mahogany table encrusted with bronze and abandoned ourselves to the Russian passion for shooting the breeze. The ladies began by detailing the history of the palace under the Soviet regime. The 1917 Revolution left its interior intact, according to my father's record of some of the things he saw there. The walls were covered with Rembrandts, Van Dycks, and Greuzes, the doorknobs were by Gouttière, the andirons by Falconet, the floors were encrusted with marquetry, and the furniture was by Roetgen, Weisveiller, Riesner, Benemann, and Jacob. The china was all antique Sèvres, most of it presented to the czar by Marie-Antoinette. When the doors of Pavlovsk were reopened shortly after the cataclysm, all these marvels were still here intact for the delectation of visitors.

Then the palace was closed again, as the dastardly regime began quietly selling off the finest pieces in exchange for cash. The Second World War broke out; the Germans occupied Pavlovsk and vengefully blew it to smithereens after failing to take Leningrad. At the liberation, nothing remained of the place but four blackened walls. Pavlovsk was well and truly dead.

But then it was revived, thanks to the tenacity and ingenuity of its curators and restorers, who luckily possessed plans and drawings of the original building. Using these, they reconstructed the palace's interior decor down to the last wainscot. Those treasures which had not been dispersed by the Soviets were brought out of hiding, and room after room Pavlovsk reemerged as it had been in the great days of the eighteenth century. Even its ghosts returned.

I savored the simplicity, facility, and freedom with which all these Russians spoke, from the highest state officials down to the friendly curators now surrounding me.

Ludmila Koval recounted that she was standing one day with one of her colleagues in the doorway to Queen Olga's salon, when they both saw a woman in gray climb the stairs, cross the room, and disappear into the corridor. They ran after her, but found nobody.

Another time, one of the junior curators was relaxing in the salon on her own. She was sitting opposite a closed door which led into a bedroom, from which there was no other exit. With time, the parquet floor had buckled, and consequently there was a gaping crack under the door. The curator's eye happened to fall on this crack, and beyond it she saw the hem of a long skirt slipping to

and fro on the far side. She called out: no reply, but still the hem moved to and fro, so she ran to the door and opened it. The room was empty. Since then, the same phenomenon has been reported by several other colleagues.

I was ready to believe that this wing of the palace, left largely undamaged by the Germans, might still be haunted, but most of the remainder had been demolished and completely rebuilt. I didn't see how the ghosts could possibly have survived. How wrong I was . . .

At the outset of the restoration work Madame A. V., who had worked at Pavlovsk for thirty-five years, was woken in the middle of the night by the jangle of the alarm. She went round the palace in search of whatever it was that had set off the bells. When she reached the Cavaliers' Room, which was the first salon to be restored, she clearly heard voices, steps, and the sounds of doors opening and closing. Not a soul was there and the reason why the alarm went off remained a mystery.

"I have no doubt it was ghosts," said Ludmila Koval. "There have been many such reports over the years."

She then claimed that without exception every one of the curators and wardens of Pavlovsk felt apprehensive about coming to this part of the museum after nightfall, and all of them had heard inexplicable noises, whispers, and rustlings in the vicinity. By common consent there was only one character capable of haunting Pavlovsk to this extent, namely the Empress Maria Feodorovna of Russia, who built the palace in the first place and created all this enchantment.

She was born a princess of Wurtemberg and was raised at Montbéliard, where she absorbed a healthy measure of French culture. She then married Grand Duke Paul of Russia, only son of Catherine the Great—who in her memoirs hinted that this heir was the bastard of her lover Saltykov. Paul was bizarre at the best of times, but when on his mother's death he ascended the throne of Russia his eccentricity became tainted with the most vicious cruelty. His favorite pastime was to drill a regiment of soldiers all day long without a break, punishing them savagely if they put a foot wrong. Several of the troopers died of floggings they received, and the story of the regiment Paul sent on foot from St. Petersburg to Siberia became legendary. On another occasion he had a rat tried, condemned to death, and executed for nibbling at one of his uniforms.

The whole Russian empire trembled before this spiteful tyrant, who seemed to have eyes and ears everywhere. Those with the means to do so went quietly away to live in exile. And even in the idyllic surroundings of Pavlovsk, Paul the First spent his time trying to catch the sentries napping.

Luckily Pavlovsk was uncongenial to the gloomy czar, who much preferred his giant barracks-palace of Gatchina. In St. Petersburg, because he thought the Winter Palace was poorly defended, he had a lugubrious pile hastily built, which he called the Michael Fortress. He was quite right to be paranoid; his excesses had provoked deep resentment, which eventually led to a giant conspiracy. Most of the plotters belonged to the most intimate circle of his courtiers and nearly all were Freemasons.

In her early years, Maria Feodorovna, the czarina, had been an attractive blond, but as the years went by she grew fat and her husband the czar turned for solace to his various mistresses. Above all, he loathed his oldest son and heir, Alexander, who was everything that he was not: a man of refinement, charm, and good looks. Eventually Paul began to threaten both his wife and his son, looking for a pretext to imprison and perhaps execute them.

Not surprisingly, therefore, Alexander gave his approval to the plotters, on the express condition that his father be forced to abdicate only, and should come to no harm. As the noose tightened around him, the czar took refuge in his brand-new blockhouse in

St. Petersburg. He then ordered Maria Feodorovna and Alexander to join him, the better to keep an eye on them.

The conspirators realized that Paul's suspicions were thoroughly aroused. They had to act immediately. Under cover of darkness, they penetrated the best-defended fortress in Russia, using keys they had somehow obtained. They then hurried silently along the corridors to the czar's apartments. Their cries of disappointment when they found the bed empty were followed by yells of triumph when Paul was found cowering behind a screen. He was given a document of abdication to sign, but this he refused angrily to do and was immediately stabbed and strangled to death.

So far the story is a well-known one. What is less well known is the fact that Alexander, whose apartments were directly below his father's, heard everything that happened. He was paralyzed with horror when the conspirators burst into his rooms to proclaim him emperor; nevertheless he made no objection. Later he came face-to-face with his mother, who was beside herself with rage, invoking her own right to the crown. But the assassins brushed Maria Feodorovna aside and carried Alexander away to meet his destiny.

When Bonaparte heard about the assassination of Czar Paul his comment was, *"Encore un coup de l'Angleterre."* In effect, the czar had recently changed alliances, abandoning England for France.

Both contemporary and later historians have roundly condemned Paul the First. Nevertheless, in the imperial pantheon within the Peter-Paul fortress, his is the only tomb which is still regularly covered with flowers, for the Russian people have always had a weird respect for madmen. Paul's successor, Alexander I, spent several years thereafter playing cat and mouse with Napoleon, being strongly advised by his mother to resist the French emperor's blandishments. Napoleon, who could not understand this, accused him of lying and called him a "grec de bas empire," by which he meant a cheat. But it was Alexander who had the last word in the War of 1812. As the vanquisher of Napoleon, he became the idol of his people and the darling of Europe.

A few years later he went away with his wife for a winter vacation in the Crimea and died shortly afterwards. Maria Feodorovna mourned him ostentatiously but before long had to face the Decembrist uprising, which came within an ace of toppling the imperial regime. Nicolas I, the brother and successor of Alexander, boldly nipped this revolution in the bud. Thereafter he set about restoring order both in his family and in the Russian empire, which was sorely in need of it; and the succeeding decades proved to be an era of

peace such as the nation had not seen for centuries.

After a few years had elapsed a rumor began to circulate in Russia to the effect that Czar Alexander's death in the Crimea had been a comprehensive fraud. Having never forgotten his own part in the murder of his father, he was supposed to have arranged his own withdrawal with a view to expiating the crime he felt he had committed. The story ran that he retired to Siberia, where he lived as a hermit in the freezing cold. Despite the indignant denials of Maria Feodorovna and the other members of the imperial family, evidence for this theory slowly but surely accumulated. The mystery eventually acquired such proportions and proved so durable that Lenin decided to clear it up once and for all by having the czar's coffin opened. There was nothing in it but stones.

So there it is. No fewer than three thoroughgoing mysteries—the identity of Paul I's true father, the exact circumstances of his assassination, and the faked death of Alexander I. All of these mysteries are centered around Maria Feodorovna.

Personally, I had always found Maria completely awful. She remained in my eyes a "fat, boring, uninteresting, whinging cow," in the words of a contemporary. So it was against my better instincts that I allowed myself to be closed into her cabinet on the ground floor at Pavlovsk.

There had been a leak in the room recently, and its treasures had been temporarily removed. Most of the space was encumbered by empty display cases layered with dust. White sheets hung across the windows. The water had stained the walls severely and only a couple of chimneypieces encrusted with multicolored marble were there to remind me of the original refined decor.

Just outside the door sat one of the palace's wardens, a toothless octogenarian; one of those babushkas who have become inseparable from Russian museums, and whose only function is to terrify and astonish all visitors.

I settled down to wait.

Here I am—"the Fat Cow."

I am here to defend the memory of the man I loved. Both in his lifetime and after his death he was remorselessly vilified. His own mother Catherine the Second launched a campaign against him, putting him through the worst suffering a man can endure . . . She was jealous. Catherine was the most celebrated woman in Europe, one of the giants of history. She had everything—beauty, success with men, intelligence, wit, authority, unlimited power, the adulation of her contemporaries. What could Catherine want of a son who she herself claimed was an abortion—ugly, stupid, ignorant, mad, and illegitimate! All these things she called him, in public, over and over again.

But I knew that her son, though he may not have been handsome, had an attraction of his own. In any case he attracted me and I loved him. He was clever, too, and much more cultivated than his mother. Her way was to bluff. She would read three lines of a book, than swear that she'd read it all. She was the sovereign of a chimera. Everything she did in her life was an illusion; she could make anybody believe anything. Raised in the poorest of courts with only a bare minimum of attendants, born in an era when it was considered unnecessary to educate girls, she learned only to keep her crass ignorance very carefully concealed.

I came into the world much later, and was surrounded by a much more cosmopolitan, French-influenced household. I was carefully educated and could read four languages fluently. My husband's education, which was even wider than mine, was perhaps less bookish; though he knew Faust by heart, his knowledge of this and other classics rested more on his sensibility than on his memory. He appreciated beauty in all its forms, and this house is the living proof of it.

He and I walked so often in the gardens below these windows that we seem almost to be walking there still, arm in arm along the avenues. My husband, who was so miserable when he had to live in his mother's shadow, somehow blossomed at Pavlovsk. She gave him this property, and on it she built the palace according to her own ideas, often in defiance of our wishes. But in spite of her meddling Pavlovsk became our exclusive world.

If I managed to do one service to my husband, it was that of teaching him to appreciate ordinary, simple, healthy pleasures. He was fated to become the sole master of a gigantic empire, commanding millions of subjects and fabulous wealth; but here he found a paradise of his own, in which he planted his garden and supervised the work of the fields. Above all, he was interested in the lives of the people in his employ. He took infinite pains on behalf of his servants and peasants. With these he was more courteous by far than with the great ones who formed his entourage, because he knew that humble people understood him better than the great ones.

In the course of time, Catherine died. My husband came to the throne, determined to work for the good of his family, his family being every soul in the empire. His reforms were revolutionary and completely disinterested. He was honest and incorruptible, though sometimes obdurate: but he knew how to listen to wise advice, and his decision to institute progress in Russia led to his downfall.

Of course his death was decided upon long before it actually took place. The problem was, how to wreck his reputation in the eyes of the people, before he was destroyed.

Paul's powerful enemies perpetuated the campaign of denigration begun by Empress Catherine. They amplified the rumors of his illegitimacy. His mother had been sufficiently diabolical as to cast doubt on his origins to his face, so that all his life he wondered if he were his father's son, or not. Night and day he tortured himself with doubts about his right to the throne, for as a bastard he should in conscience yield it to someone else with more right than he. But in this case, to whom? Because with him the dynasty would come to an end.

His prickly manner was entirely superficial, as were his sudden shifts of mood and explosions of rage. His harshness and occasional cruelty were likewise engendered by the perpetual state of uncertainty in which he lived.

After the death of Empress Catherine, I made a detailed investigation of her life and proved that my husband could not have been illegitimate. Had I discovered the contrary, I would certainly have advised him to abdicate, and he would have done so. He believed the evidence I furnished, but the evil instilled in him by his mother could not be dislodged so easily and he continued to doubt, in spite of himself. I loathed my dead mother-in-law for this deed of hers: I imagined her somewhere in hell, rejoicing in the wicked turn she had done to her only son.

Meanwhile my husband's enemies intensified their propaganda campaign against him, spreading ugly rumors such as the one about his torturing of soldiers. The truth here was simply that Paul purged the army of the parasites lodged in its highest echelons by his mother, most of whom

were her former lovers. This he did with ruthless efficiency, and the result was that our son Alexander was able to win the unexpected victory against Napoleon which remains the greatest triumph in Russian history.

It is a fact that my husband had mistresses; but I myself can claim that none of these were seriously physical passions. The liaisons, for which I was so often mocked, were no more than romantic attachments. Paul continued to love me and I loved him more than ever. I admired his tireless determination to achieve his goals, without compromise, delay, or hesitation, even though he was constantly assailed by personal doubts, threats, warnings, and betrayals. And the only refuge he had from these anxieties was this house, where he could be with his family.

The slander has it that he concealed himself behind the shutters, spying on the guards and punishing them for the slightest laxity. In reality, he simply liked to stand at the window of this room, looking out at the view and telling me how beautiful he found it.

Later on, my husband's descendants, Nicolas II and his family, also retired to the country; but their manner of doing so was entirely different from ours. Here we were isolated, but we were never cut off from the nation as they were. Even when he was in this house, surrounded by this wide delicious park, Paul listened to the murmurings of his empire. He may have been hopelessly misjudged by the historians, but the mighty

Russian people loved and understood him, and that love has survived to this day.

Although we were happy and peaceful at Pavlovsk, my husband sometimes retired to those gloomy fortresses in St. Petersburg. The appalling psychological ordeals he had undergone virtually from the hour of his birth subjected him to periodic lunatic crises. He did his best to hide these from his family and other people. When a crisis threatened, his reaction was to lock himself up, under the delusion that if he were protected behind thick walls and moats and whole regiments of soldiers, his demons could not get at him. His tragedy was that in his paroxysms he was liable to inflict the greatest harm on those he loved the most. And he knew it.

Gradually, the dangers gathered around him, and both our lives grew more circumscribed.

Paul possessed incontrovertible proof of the existence of a plot; he even knew the identities of the plotters, but still he refused to move against them. I had heard nothing but vague rumors, and didn't know enough to be of any practical assistance. Each time I urged him to strike at his enemies, he replied that there was plenty of time, and anyway he needed further proof. This was untrue: he already knew everything.

Some of the conspirators approached the czarevitch, Alexander. In the poisoned atmosphere of the court, our son dared not show by any sign or gesture that he understood their veiled allusions. Later he told me he had never assented in any way

to what was suggested, and I have no reason to doubt his word. Alexander was always completely sincere in what he said and did, but he had a horror of scenes and outbursts of anger, no doubt because he had witnessed his father's terrifying crises. All his life he maintained a front of serene equanimity, and whenever he had to say something disagreeable he vacillated shamelessly—hence the accusation of hypocrisy so often leveled at him. As his mother, I can vouch for the fact that he wasn't lying when he denied all knowledge of the plot.

Nevertheless the conspirators were crafty enough to spread the word that Alexander was in league with them. This rumor reached my husband at a time when our son's attitude toward his father was unusually critical, and Paul was much agitated. I tried to calm him down, but he wouldn't listen, and when Alexander himself arrived to pass on the little he knew of the plot, Paul sent him packing.

Most of all, Paul was exasperated because he was being taken for an idiot. One day he started muttering angrily about it, in the presence of witnesses who immediately came running to Alexander and me with the news that Paul had threatened us by name and was about to have us arrested.

He had scarcely moved into his new, unfinished Petersburg residence when he called us to join him. He was frankly lonely. The knowledge that we were under the same roof, even one as gloomy as *that, was a comfort to him, as if we had brought a little sunshine from outside.*

We found him in an appalling state. He had summoned us for help and encouragement, but we could do nothing against his lassitude. Everything he had attempted had gone awry. His reforms had raised a storm of protest: they were only to bear fruit much later. At the same time his shadowy enemies were preparing for the kill, which he no longer had the desire or the energy to avert. Morbidly, he asked a man he knew to be a conspirator if it was true that there was a plot to assassinate him, and if he (the man) was party to it. The reply came straight back that yes, it was perfectly true, and if he was a participant, it was because he meant to expose the others. This staggering lie shook Paul to the very depths; and far from being reassured, as the legend says he was, he allowed this final enormity of treason to strip away his last resistance.

What happened next was unavoidable. My husband was not killed, he merely allowed himself to die. His Christian faith forbade suicide, so he allowed his assassins to do the work for him.

The scene of his death returned to me in nightmares for the rest of my days. I heard the whispers and the footfalls; those men tried to move quietly, but they were drunk, and they kept bumping into each other, cursing and muttering as they felt their way along the passages. Like a coward, I did nothing. I knew something terrible was about to happen. I heard them smash down the door to

Paul's bedroom, the din of falling objects and upended furniture, the whoop of triumph when they found their victim. I heard his screams of pain, I knew that voice, and I heard the snarls of his killers. I couldn't move or breathe. Would they now come looking for Alexander and me, to murder us in turn? How could I warn my son? I was alone, and I could hear them.

Then the shouts died away, and my husband's shrieks ceased. It was almost a relief, though I knew what that silence meant. I am describing these thoughts at some length, but at the time they came to me all at once, in a single lightning flash. I shook off my paralysis and rushed from my room: as I might have expected, there was no servant or soldier on the scene to protect us or see to our needs. In the corridor I came face-to-face with the assassins, who insulted me and ordered me back to my bed. They were roaring in drink, and some were spattered with blood, the blood of my husband. I took no notice of them, but marched forward and was just in time to see my son being hustled away. I tried to intervene, sure that they meant to kill Alexander too—hence the stupid story that I attempted to invoke some kind of imaginary right to the succession of the czar. But Alexander quietly followed his father's murderers from the scene, and in retrospect I can see he did the right thing. He had no alternative.

The assassins were never brought to book. They were too powerful and too dangerous. Their ramifications extended through a secret society (the

Freemasons) to a great power (England), neither of which had ever shown the least scruple where power was concerned. The death of my husband was the proof, and I am quite sure the same fate would have befallen his successor had he given the least pretext. Alexander knew this and so did I. And it was I who advised him to stay the hand of justice.

For the rest of my life I stood firm. My children's father was dead, and their elder brother had assumed the burdens of state, so it was up to me to look to their interests. I saw them grow up, marry, and have children of their own. Pavlovsk

throughout that time remained a place of peace and happiness.

Then Alexander left. The secret of his end remains one of the most poignant in history, and was a terrible sorrow to me. The small daily pleasures which had made my long widowhood bearable suddenly lost their savor. I knew that the life was draining out of me and I had no particular wish to prolong the process. My time was over, and soon enough I fell ill and died. Where I am now, I see things and people in a far clearer light, and my longing for vengeance remains intact. I hope that one day I shall see Paul again.

THE WOMAN WHO DIED OF LOVE

Powderham Castle, Devon, England

L OUIS VI OF FRANCE (1081–1137) was known as Louis the Fat. He was a candid sovereign, progressive and benevolent. His reign was one of the most popular—and prosperous—of the Middle Ages.

Upon his second wife, Adelaide of Savoy, Louis begot several children, the youngest of whom was Pierre, Lord of Courtenay. Pierre went forth to the Crusade, strove manfully against the Saracens, and forged a reputation for himself as a gallant knight. From the Holy Land he carried home one of the most revered relics of Christianity, a trio of droplets of the True Blood of Christ, for which he commissioned the richest of reliquaries, now preserved at Bruges.

The House of France having not yet adopted the fleur-de-lis as its emblem, Pierre de Courtenay's pious exploit was commemorated by his adoption of what are known as "canting" or allusive armorial bearings: three red circles, in token of the drops of Christ's blood. These arms are more properly described in heraldry as "gold, three roundels gules, with a label azure."

The Sire de Courtenay had many descendants. An adventuring royal Courtenay eventually became emperor in Constantinople, and his issue reigned until 1261 over the short-lived Latin Empire which replaced Byzantium. Another, an impoverished younger son, went to seek his fortune in England, where he offered his services to the first Angevin king. He and his descendants accumulated estates, castles, titles, and important offices. But working for the English monarchs was not without its dangers, and the Courtenays, like other great families of England, had their share of beheadings and forfeited estates. Nevertheless, they always managed to rebuild their fortunes and regain their lost titles.

In modern times, the British monarchs no longer cut the heads off people who annoy or displease them, though they would probably love to; and for their own part the Courtenay earls of Devon are now content to administer the broad acres around their ancient seat of Powderham. Formerly a fortress at the disposal of the king—and on occasion a refuge from his vengeful whims—this splendid pile is the Courtenay family's principal residence. They maintain it with loving care, and in the shooting season entertain some of the world's most renowned sportsmen, for the woods and fields around are alive with all kinds of game.

Not so long ago it happened that my cousin Olympia was invited down to Powderham for a shooting weekend. Olympia is a lively girl of the smiling Mediter-

ranean type, whose elegance and grace hide great courage and an intrepid nature.

On this occasion she came with her husband, who was shooting, but since she was pregnant she was strongly advised not to go out with the guns, on account of the bumpy Land Rover rides she would certainly have to endure as the sportsmen made their way from cover to cover. Their hostess, the Countess of Devon, therefore installed Olympia in one of the great drawing rooms at Powderham, equipped her with tea, newspapers, and magazines, and hurried off in the wake of the shooting party.

Finding herself alone, Olympia looked around her. The sunlight streaming through the tall windows, the comfortable sofas, the gay springlike chintzes all combined to mitigate the enormous size of the room and its high ceiling. The atmosphere was deliciously warm and luxurious. She took up her book and settled herself to read.

But very soon it became clear to Olympia that try as she might, she could not focus her mind on the pages before her. The words and phrases seemed to dance in front of her eyes. Her thoughts veered away in all directions. Then she gradually became aware of a most disagreeable sensation, which she could not at first define; something was insinuating itself into her consciousness, something deeply unpleasant. She had no idea what this might be, or where it was coming from. She called Lady Devon's cocker spaniel, who had been left behind to keep her company. The dog trotted to her hand, and Olympia began to stroke its head abstractedly. Suddenly she felt the creature stiffen and bristle under her fingers. It turned its head and snarled, as if some hostile presence had entered the room. Olympia twisted on the cushions and glanced behind her: there was nobody there. But the little dog stood rigid, quivering with fright, before long it was howling, "howling like death," Olympia told me afterwards. Suddenly a ball of fur leapt straight at Olympia's chest, making her cry out involuntarily. This was the cat, which hitherto she hadn't noticed: now it clawed furiously at her breast, ripping her blouse. The creature's eyes were bulging from its head; like the spaniel's they were fixed on the same invisible presence.

Olympia hugged the dog to her, while the cat continued to clutch at her clothes. She shut her eyes tight. She knew that the spirit of something or someone infinitely evil and hideous was hovering close by. The room, which earlier had been flooded with sunlight, was perceptibly darkened.

Olympia, responding by instinct, murmured a simple prayer she had learned as a child. Though her eyes were still tightly closed, she sensed that the thing facing her had paused in its onward motion. As she continued to pray, little by little she felt the danger diminish and at last evaporate altogether. She opened her eyes hesitantly, shaking with terror. Nothing. No one. The dog and the cat were calm again, as if nothing had happened.

In the immediate aftermath, she dared not mention this experience to her hosts. But the following year, when she and her husband were again asked to stay at Powderham, there was no question of Olympia staying behind when the shooting party set off for the day. Even so, when she saw the house again she could not resist asking Lady Devon in an offhand manner if there were any ghosts on the premises. "Nonsense!" was the brisk reply.

After hearing what Olympia had to say, Justin and I drove down to Powderham to see for ourselves. It was a fine spring day, though I have to admit that, rain or shine, Devonshire always puts me powerfully in mind of the Hound of the Baskervilles. Turning off a country road lined with dry stone walls, we entered the broad, noble park of Powderham.

Rhododendrons and other flowering shrubs grew in clusters on the smooth lawns ahead of us. Long avenues of ancient trees wound through meadows dotted with grazing horses; Powderham that afternoon epitomized the magnificence of a great English estate. Ahead of us, on a gentle rise in the land, stood the castle, venerable and huge, rendered even more melodramatic by its Victorian turrets and battlements, and in the distance gleamed the sea. Over the keep flew the banner of the Courtenays: gold, three roundels gules, with a label azure.

The military grimness of the exterior gave no hint of the luxury and refinement within. The marble hall, the antechambers, the White Salon, the Blue Salon, the principal library, the second library, the music room, the great banqueting hall—between them, they offered a complete overview of the decorative arts of the seventeenth and eighteenth centuries, from richly ornamented Baroque to the stark elegance of the neoclassical style. The furniture, built by local craftsmen but easily worthy of the great masters of London, showed how well the lords of Powderham had learned to discover hidden talent and give it a chance to flower. Against the finely carved wood panels and on the walls hung with damask, an admirable series of portraits commemorated the successive occupants of the castle.

Lord Courtenay, Lady Devon's son, appeared to show us around. He walked with a pronounced stoop, as if to offset his great height. Courteous and shy, he seemed ever so slightly discomfited in the role of guide. We followed him up the great stair-

case with its rococo panels, bathed in sunshine from a broad skylight above. On the landing, we turned into a small antechamber leading through to the apartments and bedrooms. This room was paneled in dark oak: the only furnishings were a heavy table on which stood a curious bronze object brought home from an imperial punitive expedition, which Lord Courtenay told us had once crowned the palanquin of the dowager empress of China, and, beside the table, two glass bowls containing tropical seashells. Beyond the single, narrow Gothic window, with its dark fringe of ivy, stretched the sunny park, rich with the colors of spring, which seemed to belong to a world totally apart from this cold, austere cubicle. "Here we are," murmured Lord Courtenay, and I understood that we were standing in the haunted room.

The story as he told it began in 1939. A general blackout was then effective throughout Britain. Lord Courtenay's mother, the Countess of Devon, accompanied by his French governess, Mademoiselle Irène Collard, decided to undertake an official tour of the castle to make sure that all the windows had been properly darkened. When they reached the antechamber, they found that the shutters had not been closed. They shifted the table in front of the window along with the two glass bowls with the

seashells, and swung back the wooden flaps which opened into the room. Then the two ladies retired to bed, satisfied that everything was snugly camouflaged from the prowling Luftwaffe.

The next night, Mademoiselle Collard did the rounds alone: and before long she was tapping at the door of Lady Devon's boudoir with the news that she "couldn't close" the shutters in the antechamber, which appeared to have been opened by one of the maids.

This was hardly surprising: Mlle. Collard was a tiny person, and the window was very tall. Lady Devon went to the room forthwith, grasped one of the offending shutters, and heaved. It wouldn't budge. After several vain attempts, she examined the wood more closely and was stunned to discover that each panel had been securely nailed against the inner frame of the window embrasure. Even more strange, the nails appeared to be very old and rusty, as if this operation had been carried out many years before.

Lady Devon summoned the estate carpenter.

"Who on earth came here this morning and nailed back these shutters, which I myself closed yesterday night?"

The man stared at her in astonishment.

"Your ladyship, them shutters has been nailed to the frame for upwards of thirty years."

"I repeat, I closed them with my own hands last night."

"Well, madam, you can see for yourself they can't have been prized off any time recently."

"But why on earth were they nailed up to begin with?"

"It was old Lord Devon, your ladyship's father-in-law, who had it done."

And then the carpenter lowered his voice. He explained that at one time the servants had complained that it was impossible to open the shutters in the antechamber. They muttered about "devil's work," and by common accord decided that it was best to stay away from "that room" altogether. Lady Devon had to accept her carpenter's explanation; nevertheless, she was sufficiently struck by the circumstance to make a note of it on her fine monogrammed writing paper.

Decades after, it was this same Lady Devon who replied "Nonsense!" to my cousin Olympia's inquiry about ghosts.

So what did Lord Courtenay himself think? It was clear that the subject was not one he was over-eager to discuss. But he did mention that his dogs hated to pass through here, and that as a child he instinctively moved a trifle faster when he had to cross the antechamber on his way to see his parents.

"And do the tourists who come here react in any way?"

"You'll have to ask Michael about that," said Lord Courtenay. Apparently Michael Thomasson, the official guide to Powderham Castle, had indeed noted some peculiar reactions on his tours.

Michael was an energetic young man, with a lively tongue and a quick, inquiring eye. His hair was prematurely gray and he seemed widely cultured. Above all he knew every detail of the castle and its history, and was genuinely interested in ghosts and all other aspects of the supernatural. Indeed I judged him to be unusually sensitive in these domains, like myself.

Michael had begun working at Powderham a few years earlier. One day he happened to be standing in the courtyard with another guide when a couple of tourists sprinted past them in the direction of the exit. Supposing, not unnaturally, that the sprinters might have stolen some object from the house, the two guides barred their way. But the reason for their flight turned out to be terror, not larceny. The tourists fought their way madly past, bawling that they'd seen "a hand coming out of the wall" in the second-floor antechamber.

On another occasion, Michael was conducting a guided tour for a group that included a pregnant woman. When they entered the antechamber, the woman let out a shriek, gasping that she felt the onset of labor. She was carried into a bedroom, and a

doctor was summoned. The pains were acute—unbelieveably so given that after a couple of hours it became clear that the whole thing was a false alarm. Shortly afterwards, Michael was showing yet another group around, this time through the rose garden, when a girl suddenly pointed upward at the Gothic window of the antechamber. "Look," she said, "there's a woman up there watching us!" The others stared: they could see nothing. "I see her as clear as I see you," said the girl, "and very nasty she looks too."

But Michael knew that it was quite impossible that any mortal could be in the antechamber at that hour.

It was a common occurrence, he said, that cameras which had worked perfectly well in other rooms in the castle completely failed to operate in the antechamber.

From his observations Michael concluded that the most likely people to react to the room were women and adolescents. Many felt faint, and some became nauseated to the point of actually vomiting. In the course of one out of every two visits, Michael found he had to assist at least one person taken violently ill on entering the antechamber.

Not so long ago, he had singled out a man of about fifty, going round the castle with a group, who seemed to know a great deal about the history of the castle. Michael, who

has an excellent memory for faces, was virtually certain he had never seen this person. Intrigued, he asked the man if he had been to Powderham before, receiving no answer beyond an enigmatic smile. When the visit was over, the stranger took Michael aside. He was here, he said, because he had been directed to come by "spirits." Throughout the tour, he had felt himself "accompanied by the third Lord Courtenay," the eighteenth-century one, a remarkable man and a great patron of the arts who had contributed more than anyone else to the embellishment of the castle, but whose life had been ruined by a celebrated scandal. This shade had whispered in his ear the very precise details which had so impressed Michael. The stranger explained that his mission was to free the soul imprisoned in this room, and thus deliver the castle from its baleful influence. Michael, in spite of everything, remained skeptical: but at this point the stranger made certain remarks about Michael—and particularly about his childhood—which nobody else could possibly have known. Then he turned on his heel and left. Michael never had sight nor sound of him again.

Anyway, there was no question in my own mind that the room was haunted: and so very unpleasantly haunted that one had to resist a strong inclination to turn tail and run.

I asked Lord Courtenay what was on the floor below.

"Odd you should ask that. At the end of the last century, when they were putting in the plumbing, a walled-in room was discovered down there. It was quite empty, but the strangest thing was it didn't feature in the plans of the castle, and no archive ever mentioned that any room was blocked off. My grandparents converted it into a bathroom."

"How do we get there?"

Lord Courtenay led us to a staircase so narrow and dark that I hadn't noticed it earlier. Cut into the wall, it went straight down to a tiny white-painted room containing a bath and a small table. At this point I asked to be left alone.

"Today is Friday the Thirteenth. Perhaps that may make a difference," suggested Lord Courtenay, half-joking.

"I'm not in the least superstitious," I told him stoutly, "and nor, to my certain knowledge, are ghosts."

Still, I have to confess that I felt deep regret, even dread when I saw the others file back up the stairs.

I closed the bathroom door and sat on the table, considering the bare little space, which on the face of it held no mystery whatever. Nevertheless my eyes were irresistibly drawn to the darkest corner underneath the stairs. Walking down the narrow steps, I had already felt a strong sensation of revulsion: this I had managed briefly to put out of my head, but now it returned with much greater force and insistency. At the same time I was aware of a kind of appeal . . . and now I had the impression of sinking in quicksand, of being slowly drawn toward something hideous and unnameable. Something was weighing heavily upon me, preventing me from either moving or reacting. I had to make an effort to rise and walk across to the narrow window, and an even mightie one to open it, given that nobody seemed to have touched it in scores of years.

The sea air and the spring sunshine came flooding in around me, but even these weren't enough to dissipate my cold sense of malaise. Now I felt the beginnings, faint but definite, of nausea. I remembered what Michael had told me: but unlike the ghost's victims of choice I was neither a pregnant woman nor an adolescent. Still the need to vomit grew within me. As to the power that menaced, it was all the time gaining in precision, and seemed about to take a definite, perceptible form. It surrounded me, penetrated me. I had to get out; but something more powerful than my own will seemed to hold me back.

Somehow I managed to pull open the door and climb the steps. It was as if I had something vaguely defined, yet horrible, close behind me, which followed on my heels into the little antechamber above. All I wanted at that moment was to escape the danger, and too bad if I had no ghost encounter to relate about Powderham.

On my way out, I turned back to take one last look at that cursed room. And at that moment I saw, barely visible in the wood paneling, another door. Instead of making good my escape, as I had intended, a sudden intuition led me to retrace my steps. I opened this new door, and found that it gave on to a staircase even narrower than that of the bathroom, which led upward to the floor above. Slowly I climbed the high steps, ducking my head to enter another tiny room, exactly above the antechamber.

The room contained nothing but a single rusty iron bed, a worm-eaten wardrobe, and some cardboard boxes. It was clear that nobody had come in here for decades, for the slender window embrasure was choked with cobwebs.

I had come suspicious but impelled by invincible curiosity, watchful and determined to stay for a moment only. But all of a sudden I felt inexplicably reassured, relaxed, even protected. I lingered, savoring this moment of serenity which contrasted so

utterly with the horror I had just endured in the rooms below. I looked at the contents of the boxes, stuffed haphazardly with old, yellowing invitation cards. I opened the wardrobe, and found it contained a few dresses from the 1920s, dusty and moth-eaten. All of these things should by rights have made me melancholy, but not a bit of it: all I could feel was an impression of calm, a growing conviction that I was welcome.

I sat down on the bedsprings and waited.

In the mid-nineteenth century, England's aristocracy governed England, and England, to all intents and purposes, governed the world. While a lackluster royal court lapsed into bourgeois manners under Queen Victoria, the nation's great families enjoyed themselves and spent money like water. They possessed colossal fortunes and estates that covered whole counties. According to the results of periodic elections, they took turns to occupy the highest offices of the state. They only come to London for a short but fast-paced season, preferring to live in the country. Each of these families owned several great country houses, which were crammed with priceless pictures, furniture, and other apparently inexhaustible collections. The seasons dictated the migrations of these thrice-blessed people, which were as unvarying as the migrations of wildfowl.

Powderham was an autumn residence. The men went off shooting at an early hour each morning,

and returned in the evening to talk about the self-same subject. Tall and strong, they sported bushy side-whiskers and smoked cigars. They invariably dressed for dinner. During the day, their women stayed en neglig´e, only occasionally venturing forth on short walks. Most of the time, they gathered in one drawing room or another to play cards, chat, laugh, and gossip. In the evenings, they put on their best things, namely uncomfortable crinolines painfully cinched at the waist. They prided themselves on their huge, magnificent jewels, whose brightness set off their delicately perfumed arms and shoulders.

Literally hundreds of servants assured the creature comforts of the lords of Powderham and their guests—and among these servants was a slender young girl with auburn curls. This girl also had a sweet triangular face, large brown eyes, a full mouth, and small, perfect, very white teeth: by any reckoning, she was a beauty.

Not so long ago, I was a servant in this house. The uniform became me very well, I think. Our liveries had different details, depending on our rank. The height of my cap, for example, showed that I was the chambermaid of the mistress of the house: and indeed my mistress was a lovely creature, full of life and gaiety, who confided in me and told me about her innocent flirtations. In fact, she and her husband, who were both young, were very much in love with one another. My room was here, under the eaves, close to my mistress's bedroom—sleeping here, I could be on hand whenever she needed me.

Everybody knew that the little antechamber was haunted, and there wasn't one of us who didn't walk a little faster when we had to pass through it. As to the room below, it had been converted into a bathroom, but was never used. Nobody cared to go down there. There was a kind of understanding that perhaps it would be best not to hazard ourselves on those stairs. Some things are best left alone.

I can shed very little light on the mystery of that tiny bathroom. I only know it is a very terrible one, concerning a woman who committed a crime so atrocious that the horror surrounding her own end was a trifle by comparison. People shouldn't trouble themselves about her, nor should they go near, for her longing is to drag down into the pit all those who do. She tries to stamp on mortals the same black horror that once engulfed her. She is magnificent in her way, the very distillation of evil. During her lifetime, she was an instrument for the darkest forces, and has remained so beyond the grave.

I am her counterpart; her opposite, you could say. I didn't live here all year round, since I went everywhere with my mistress. Powderham stayed empty and silent for many months of the year, but during the shooting season it was full of life, activity, and gaiety. There was just as much fun and excitement below stairs as among the gentry, because at that time of year the servants were joined by the various gamekeepers, who came in at the end of each day's shooting to relax, talk, and drink with the rest of us. One year there was a newcomer: he was handsome, tall, and smooth-chinned, with blue eyes and unruly brown hair. I liked his generous laughter: I liked his intense, sad glances. He let those glances linger on me and soon enough I fell in love. He was younger than me by a year; his name was Henry. I was Mary.

Every night we lay together in this bedroom. He slipped up here while the gentry were at table and waited while I did the evening chores for my mistress. She may have got wind of our affair: anyway, she kept me back as little as possible, and sometimes even let me go before her toilet was done.

I was the playful type, always laughing and playing tricks. But Henry was a melancholy man. The gulf standing between his ambitions and tastes, and his real condition in life, made him glum. I wanted him to love life, as I did—and when we were together in this room we did just so. We resolved to stay together always, and we laid plans for the future. Henry hoped to leave the estate and find work in town. He knew he had the ability to take up an interesting profession and earn enough money to keep us. But meanwhile we had only our wages.

At the end of the shooting season we had to separate. Henry stayed at Powderham, gamekeeping, and I followed the family to their main house. We bowed to the inevitable: we promised we would write letters; we would be reunited the following *year. Maybe Henry would find some way to pay me a visit in the meantime. We parted with the hope that we would soon be married.*

Shortly after our separation, I found that I was with child. This changed everything. I resolved that we would be married anyway and continue in our places until we had saved enough money to live together. The situation was not unusual for people in our circumstances, and I was sure I could count on my mistress's kindness to bring us together as often as possible.

So I wrote to Henry. I awaited his reply with impatience, with all the confidence I had placed in him. But no reply came, and as the days passed I began to doubt. What if he had decided to shirk his responsibilities? Had I been wrong about him all along? Yet from the bottom of my heart I knew he loved me and would not abandon me.

Yet the days and weeks passed, and it became clear that no reply would come. What was to become of me? What could I do? I would have tried, had I been able, to curse him and convince myself that my love was dead—but I could not.

Then at last a letter reached me. It was written not by Henry but by one of his friends, who knew of our affair.

Henry was dead.

Despite his strong frame, his health was fragile. He had been taken by a virulent sickness for which there was no cure. For a month he had lain delirious, in agony, and throughout that month he had repeated my name, over and over. He died calling to me, while I, far away, was doubting him.

Henry was gone, and with him all the purpose went out of my life. I went to my mistress, and without a trace of shame I told her that I was with child. There was no question of my remaining in service, but instead of chiding me that kindly, generous woman endowed me with an ample pension. And so I left: not for a moment did I consider going to my family, or to Henry's. As I well knew, in their straitened circumstances his parents could not help a girl who had not even been their son's wife; and I was sure that my own puritanical family would turn away from me in horror.

So I went back to the neighborhood of Powderham, drawn there by my memories of Henry. I found a small but comfortable cottage. The villagers were very sympathetic to me, and I settled down to await the birth of my baby. My time came, and I endured the pains in the knowledge that I would soon hold Henry's child in my arms. But the child, a boy, was stillborn. It had not survived the grief that had gnawed at me throughout those months.

Afterward, the villagers stopped coming to see me. I never thought to kill myself, for Henry would never have wanted that. I just let myself slip away. If you wish to die as much as I did, all you need do is call and wait a little while, and

death will answer. The life went out of my soul the day I heard of Henry's passing; now, with his baby dead, it drained from my heart.

The sun was hot that summer. Through the window of the bedroom where I lay, and through the open door, drifted the scent of flowers; I listened to the droning insects and the birdsong. As death came closer, so did the presence of Henry, which grew so strong that I could almost see him by me. I died on a beautiful summer day; nobody came until a week later, when my body was found still uncorrupted, my face still illuminated by a smile.

I died with a great sadness in my heart, and it was this sadness that stranded me. I have been in this room ever since. I was seldom here in my lifetime, nor did I die here, but it was in this bed that my destiny was sealed. I am only a modest presence by comparison with the woman of the antechamber, who wields such awful power. Yet is she really so much stronger than I, who give those who enter this little room nothing but a sensation of serenity and well-being?

I am happy to linger here, in this place where I was so happy in my life. Many ghosts regret their lives on earth. But I, despite my misfortune, once knew the deepest happiness life can afford, if only for a moment.

I know that one day I shall see Henry again. Those who have loved each other are always reunited.

When the spell was broken, it was already evening. The tourists and the guides were gone, and even the owners of Powderham had driven back to London. I found myself the only mortal in the house. I rose, looked back one last time at the little bedroom, and left on tiptoe. I made my way down the narrow steps, and walked unhurriedly across the deadly antechamber. The hideous, threatening presence was still lurking in the shadows, but now I knew myself beyond its reach.

I passed down the main staircase, crossed the great darkening rooms, and quit the house, closing the heavy oak door softly behind me. The empty courtyard outside was bathed in a gentle light of evening.

MONTAGUE AND CAPULET
IN PROVENCE

Château de Lagnes, Provence, France

THE LOVE MATCH BETWEEN Catherine and her château has lasted for a full thirty years. On that day in 1963 when it was revealed to her, I imagine that she was driving along just as Justin and I were this September morning, on the road from Avignon to Gordes. Only there was probably a good deal less traffic then, and the holiday houses would have been far fewer.

At the time, Catherine was an actress, full of youth and talent, with a bright future. Moreover, she was the perfect double of one of the most famous of French actresses, Mme. Favart, whose reincarnation she almost believed she was.

To her left, overlooking the village of Lagnes slightly off the main road, was a looming mass of yellow stone. Catherine was attracted to this as if by a magnet and before long she found herself driving toward it along a deserted village street. She left her car at the bottom of the hill and took the rocky path leading up to the gate of the fortress.

The iron gateway visible today probably didn't exist then, and the house was open to the four winds. The harmoniously arranged planes of stone and the elaborately designed terraces were also far in the future: all Catherine saw in 1963 was a chaos of rubble. The great cypress trees stood sentinel before the buildings which, thirty years ago, were in imminent danger of collapse, with goats

picking their way right up to the top floor. And finally, the dog Titus who came out to welcome Justin and me was as yet unborn; the figure who met Catherine was the owner himself, dramatically framed by one of the posterns.

This owner was about to sell the castle to a pig dealer. But Catherine, though she hadn't even had time to go over it in detail, was already completely under its spell. She managed to win a stay of execution of one week. Of course, she hadn't two sous to rub together; but she convinced her mother to help her, passed the hat around among her theater friends, and borrowed cash from everyone who would lend. In short, she managed to assemble the money required, bought the Château de Lagnes, and immediately set to work on it virtually unaided.

Morning to night, she lugged heavy rubble from A to B, mixing mortar, shoring up walls, and erecting wooden structures. However, before deciding to buy she had taken one or two elementary precautions. Armed with photographs, she went for the first time in her life to consult a clairvoyant, a former seamstress living in a wretched sixth-floor apartment. The latter strongly encouraged her in her enterprise, but cautioned her against the ghosts haunting the castle—in particular the one whose mortal remains were lodged in a buttress of the chapel.

"He was a monster, a horror. He bled his victims . . . "

Intrigued, Catherine went down to consult the village archives, only to discover that they had been sold off by the kilo to a vendor of *pommes frites*, as wrapping for his product. There remained the departmental records, and here Catherine struck gold.

It all took place in the reign of the Bon Roi René, in the fifteenth century. Unfortunately, that jolly monarch spent much of his time at the wars, far removed from his beloved Provence: which, in his absence, fell prey to marauding robbers. From time to time, one of these robbers would be apprehended by the constabulary, and so it happened that one named Maltostens fell into the hands of the law. The judge quickly understood that the man before him was only a minor catch, and had him vigorously put to the question, in the manner of that time, with a view to extracting the name of the robber chief, Pierre Archilon; which being accomplished, an order was issued to seek out and apprehend the said Archilon.

But Archilon was already in custody at the Château de Lagnes, whose lord had thrown him into prison for some small crime committed on his domain. At the request of his suzerain, the Seigneur de Lagnes duly handed over his captive to the Justice of Provence.

Archilon was an important catch, a man

who stripped travelers of their belongings and butchered them impartially, a blasphemer who mocked at religion, and a pimp who kidnapped honest women and sold them into prostitution. Condemned to hang from a hempen cord, he was executed directly, and the land was delivered from his depredations. All thanks to the Seigneur de Lagnes, who had had the bright idea of arresting him in the first place.

The case did not, however, rest there. The trial had brought to light a number of curious facts. This Seigneur de Lagnes, who was well known in the region, was the son of one of the highest dignitaries in the court of King René, and it transpired that the seigneur was in fact an intimate friend of Archilon the Bandit. There were even witnesses who suggested he had transformed his castle into an open refuge for Archilon's band of robbers, from which fact it might be deduced that he had played a part in the latter's business activities. But no judge was rash enough to suggest this, and the Seigneur de Lagnes was in no way troubled.

"All the others were caught and killed," explained Catherine. "But the Seigneur de Lagnes, because of his high birth, his titles, and his high-placed friends, escaped scot-free."

The name of the Seigneur de Lagnes was Charles Saignet. As it turned out, the clairvoyant had correctly described him as a black villain, but he did not "bleed" (*saign-er*) his victims, he was merely called Saignet.

The clairvoyant added that, for the tranquillity of the castle and of Catherine herself, the remains of this monster should be dug up and buried elsewhere. Following the directions given to her, Catherine found in one wall of the chapel a reinforcement that appeared to have been hastily blocked up. She began to dig there, in imminent danger of being crushed by the crumbling ceiling. She persevered until she came on a kind of tunnel from which issued an icy cold draft: here she slipped and was nearly crushed at the foot of the wall. After this she passed the job on to a team of professional archaeologists, who soon discovered fourteen pots dating from the fifth century B.C., containing traces of charcoal. These pots were distributed around a casket containing human bones, and the way they were distributed left little doubt that an exorcism had been performed. Catherine transferred the bones into another box—it seems fairly certain that they were Saignet's—sprinkled them with holy water, and threw them into the Rhône from the bridge at Avignon.

It had been made very clear to Catherine by the clairvoyant that she would have to expiate the sins of Saignet, and although she was initially skeptical, she had ample time to bemoan this fact in the years that followed. The dead and the living swarmed upon her in about equal numbers, making her life a calvary. She had barely moved into what was little more than a converted corner of the ruin when she had the disagreeable sensation, several nights in succession, that somebody was trying to wring her neck. When she woke up, her throat was bruised and sore. Later, her fields and trees (and only hers) were swept by fire. Stones dropped away from walls she had just rebuilt, for no apparent reason, for she is a perfectly competent mason. She was refused building permissions and authorizations that were completely justifiable. But still she persevered, stubbornly remaining at Lagnes, until that awful night . . .

Catherine went out to a play at the Festival d'Avignon and returned late to see her château burning merrily in the distance. By the time the firemen stopped the blaze, her eighteen years of hard work had been obliterated. Would she give up at last?

Not for a moment was she tempted to do so. On the contrary, she recovered in record time, set to work, and resuscitated the castle all over again. Again luck turned against her, when her chest was crushed in an accident and she was condemned to months of pain and immobility. But none of this daunted her, for she was fully aware of the cumulative curse that weighed on her castle, and was determined to get the better of it.

We left the chapel where the bones of Charles Saignet had been unearthed, and wandered off along the irregularly paved alleys that led past the buildings and ramparts. Something about all this struck me forcibly.

"It looks to me as if there was not one, but two castles here."

"There certainly were. At the outset Lagnes was a 'coseigneurie,' meaning it belonged to two rival families who never stopped fighting and murdering each other. Now have a look at this . . ."

Catherine led the way to the top floor, to a small sunlit room with plaster cavities all along its walls, some of which were hollow and some filled in. Was it a pigeon house, I inquired. Not at all.

"They used to mix the ashes of the Vaudois people killed in the Wars of Religion with plaster, and stick them in these cavities."

Apparently Lagnes attracted the attention of the sinister Baron des Adrets, in the times when Catholics and Protestants were murdering each other with unparalleled ferocity. Des Adrets, a specialist in all forms of horror and savagery who was Catholic or Protestant just as it suited him, put no fewer than 240 people to the sword in the village of Lagnes alone. The women were carefully disemboweled, the children spitted and roasted to death, and the mutilated corpses of the men were fed to the swine.

After a moment's hesitation, Catherine then admitted us to her office, a high-ceilinged room charmingly cluttered with cassettes, books, papers, and clothes. Here

she showed us an aperture leading off the fireplace, in which a hoard of gold pieces had been found—well before her time, alas.

She told us she had always felt a bit of a presence here. One evening she brought an actress friend home and the two of them were watching *King Kong*—the first and best version—on the television. Because it was slightly chilly the two women had covered their knees with a rug. Suddenly the friend felt something warm and wet spreading over her thighs and legs, and a powerful stench of urine filled the room. A ghost was pissing on her.

The ghosts of Lagnes weren't all nasty ones, though; on this point even the clairvoyant had been reassuring. It happened that Catherine's father, before he would agree to let her go into the theatrical profession, insisted that she learn a manual craft, with the result that she found out all about the manufacture of faience. One day the curator of the Papal Palace at Avignon asked her to re-create tiles like those in the old floors there. After months of effort, Catherine achieved a result she was happy with, and the delighted curator ordered tiles in very large quantities.

Shortly afterwards, looking through the archives, Catherine found out that her castle had belonged to Jean Tescherie da Podio in the late Middle Ages. This great lord and merchant had been one of the commissioners of the Pont d'Avignon, and had furnished the original paving tiles for the Papal Palace, which strangely resembled the ones Catherine had just invented. Later still, a learned friend sent her a copy of the marriage contract of this benevolent predecessor, which had turned up in a chest at Carpentras. Putting two and two together, Catherine concluded that the clairvoyant's benevolent ghost might be that of Jean Tescherie da Podio.

In the course of her restoration work at Lagnes, Catherine frequently discovered things which encouraged her to keep going. She never dug up any treasure, but there was no lack of other elements to spark her imagination. For example, the clairvoyant had mentioned "three orange flowers," and at one point she dug up a stone escutcheon bearing the emblem of three orange flowers under a pile of rubble. This was the coat of arms of Laura, Petrarch's muse, to whom Lagnes had once belonged.

In Catherine's opinion, Petrarch's Laura wasn't Laura de Nova at all. "That's stuff and nonsense, a Renaissance lie designed to flatter François Ier. The real Laura lived here in this château, and still haunts it in a rather nice way." In support of this theory, she showed me quantities of dusty volumes: but as far as I was concerned the best evidence was supplied by the poet himself, in sonnet 293: "This tree which I possess wears the golden colours of the East, and the perfume in its fruit and flowers and leaves is the scent in which the orange excels above all others. Such is sweet Laura, in whom all beauty and all virtues live perpetually . . . "

To give beauty and virtue to her castle, Catherine can also count on the gifts of her friends—for example, the armorial bearings, in stone, of the Dullins, given to her by the famous French actor of that name when his family home was demolished. Catherine was Dullin's pupil before she worked with Vilar and Planchon; and she was also good friends with Ionesco and Albert Camus, who wanted to buy Lagnes well before she did. In the event, Catherine has sacrificed her own career to save Lagnes from ruin. She lives alone, with a few pets. This is the life she has chosen for herself, and she is not always charitable with visitors who come to disturb it. A cultivated woman who speaks very elegant French, she seems to possess indomitable energy. Her château is quite enough for her, she claims; if she needs to communicate with other beings, she can do so with a whole legion of ghosts, whom she often finds much more agreeable company than living people.

And it is true that despite the supernatural presences "felt" by Catherine and her friends, in the last analysis Lagnes is not at all a frightening place. The sunshine, the fabulous view of the region, the crystalline air, the harmonious proportions of the restored rooms, the subtle gradations of the terraces, and the goldenness of the stone all come together to create an atmosphere which is bright, warm, and welcoming.

And this was exactly what I told Catherine. But also I asked for some time alone in the attic.

"The attic?" she exclaimed. "Why, there are no ghosts *there* . . ."

Of course ghosts are real, but those who believe in them too passionately, and imagine they sense their presence everywhere, end up by creating them from scratch. Their fantasy can even be so strong that they transmit it to others. Thus, through the power of an illusion, ghosts are born, live, and die which are truly no more than ghosts of ghosts, entirely bound to the psychic state of those who invent them.

Other people are naturally negative; they see things all disturbed, even though they are not intrinsically bad. In this way they emit the waves which are at the origin of most of the manifestations attributed to ghosts, and of the nonsense talked about them. The ghosts created by the living are far worse than real ghosts, but the living themselves are worst of all. We ghosts exist in solitude, like prisoners. We lack the equipment to frighten. And when the living claim to have encountered aggressive and dangerous ghosts, all they have really done is come face-to-face with themselves.

Long ago, there were two castles on this rock, sited very close together. Both belonged to the same

family, but eventually the property was divided and subsequent marriages took the two towers out of the original line, leaving two rival clans facing each other, bitter enemies as only neighbors can be. The original cause of the quarrel was soon forgotten as their mutual hatred began to feed on itself. Each family clung to its own castle, and thrived on its loathing for the other.

Their struggles were waged through chicanery, lawsuits, proxies, thefts, and even kidnappings, engineered in such a manner that those responsible were never brought to book. Campaigns of slander and denunciations to the authorities kept this pot boiling more surely than any bombardment.

My name was Laura. I was born not far from here, and I was a tomboy. As a child I would vanish into the countryside all day long with the poor folk who were my chosen companions. I brought back herbs, wild fruits, and sweet woods.

As a very young girl, I was betrothed to the heir of one of the castles. He was handsome and rich. I had no fortune and wasn't pretty either. He married me for my name. It was an arranged marriage, but it gratified me because I liked him.

The night of our wedding, after the ceremony, we returned to the castle for a family banquet. In the same manner as a knight is given his spurs, a magus receives his consecration, or a member of a secret society is initiated by the ordeals that lead to knowledge, I was initiated into the hatred which divided us from our neighbors. This was my wedding gift. I quickly perceived that it was stealing my husband away from me; although he was neither vindictive nor rancorous by nature, he

was entirely obsessed by the rivalry between the two clans. I did my best to free him of this obsession, but could not.

And yet the ogres who so occupied our minds were invisible to me. I had never seen them. For generations, the two clans had publicly pretended the other did not exist, while spying on each other constantly.

My curiosity was aroused. I wished to see our enemies. There was no question of venturing onto their lands. Could I catch sight of them in the village, at Mass, at the fairs, perhaps? Impossible, for both sides had lookouts who kept an eye on the others' movements and made sure there were no chance encounters.

There matters rested for a while, until I began to revert to the habits of my childhood and went wandering in the maquis alone, as I used to do before I married.

One day I met on the path a young man with a face so sweet he might have been a woman. Both of us realized immediately we were in the presence of a member of the enemy tribe. He carried a catapult: he was after birds. He stared at me with astonished blue eyes, as if he thought I might turn into a witch at any moment. Then we went our separate ways.

I let a few days pass, then returned to the same place, and there he was again with his catapult. We both smiled, but almost immediately he seemed to shrink at his own audacity. No doubt the aura of mystery surrounding my name made me thoroughly attractive.

We finally spoke. I took the lead by curtseying

and giving him my name, Laura. "Chrétien," he responded, and bowed low. I immediately asked him to show me how to use the catapult, and with this our friendship began.

In an atmosphere of pervasive hatred, this friendship was a comfort to both of us. I could not hate this young man, nor he me. And in a way I enjoyed taking this small revenge over my husband's family, whom I found so harsh and stubborn. Chrétien was attractive and full of enthusiasm, and neither of us mentioned the feud between our clans.

Then came the day when he kissed me clumsily as we sat side by side, then drew back, apparently horrified by what he had done.

He did not come for the next three days, but on the fourth day he returned, having fallen madly in love with me in the interval. Despite his inexperience, he learned the gestures of love very quickly—even though I refused to become his mistress. As a result he was unhappy, and at last I managed to blind myself to the danger of a passion made all the more consuming by the obstacles standing in its way. The dalliance pleased me, but all the time his desire grew, and before long I was faced with a dilemma. Should I yield myself to him, or should I break off our friendship?

I never had time to decide, for one day as we lay on the yellow grass, locked in each other's arms, a group of hunters came upon us. They were Chrétien's uncles and cousins and his elder brother. I can still hear their shouts of triumph. They laid hands on me and hustled me away to the great hall of their castle. Then they summoned all the others of their family, their servants and vassals, and Chrétien's brother mocked me, saying again and again, "Behold the whore!" Chrétien himself was gone. I suppose they had locked him up somewhere apart. For years I had longed to look upon our enemies and had imagined romances about them, but now that I was in their power I found little to admire. They also committed the ultimate perfidy of _not_ holding me captive, for after they had exhibited and humiliated me, they sent me home.

When the gate of their castle had closed behind me, I made my way round the hill in the direction of our own main entrance. I was sorely tempted as I did so to turn away into the maquis and never return again, but for some reason I did not. The news had already filtered through, and I found my husband's whole clan silently assembled in the main hall, just as it always was when my father-in-law sat in justice on his vassals. My husband stared at me as if I were a corpse, and disgust was written on the faces of the others. Then my father-in-law motioned to the women to take me to another room, while the men decided what should be done with me. No one spoke to me; at intervals the women came and went with news of the deliberations, which they repeated loudly enough for me to hear. The choices were to repudiate me altogether, to lock me up in a convent, or to imprison me. My husband said nothing in my defense. Finally my father-in-law made his decision. He had always had a soft spot for me, and now he decreed that I should be detained in an apartment and never allowed to leave the castle. I was brought

back into the great hall to hear this sentence pronounced, after which my father-in-law personally conducted me to the attic, which at that time was divided into small rooms.

I was allowed to walk within the castle walls, but nobody was permitted to look at me or address a single word to me. As soon as I appeared, those who had formerly been my family turned their faces away. I had rather remain in my attic, and before long I ceased to go out. They treated me like they treated the clan who were their enemies: they made as if I didn't exist.

When I went down to church on Sundays, the village people shrank from me. My father-in-law, in trying to spare me pain, had made my punishment far worse than any physical torture. The years passed and nothing changed; I was a leper, and my husband ignored me like all the rest. When my father-in-law died, I vaguely hoped that my lot would improve, but it did not.

As for Chrétien, I learned what happened to him from a woman of the family, who related it to another in a voice loud enough for me to hear. He was sent away to the Crusades, where he died, perhaps of disease, perhaps in battle with the Saracens.

The hatred did not come to me for a while. First I had to void myself of despair, before hate could take its place. When it came, it was very sudden, and it turned against them the very sentiment they had tried to graft on me. I set myself to hate them, and thereafter their enemy was both within and without the castle walls. My hatred sustained me, becoming my companion and my reason for living. It was as silent as the silence they had inflicted upon me, and I came to attribute to it the power of inflicting deadly harm. Storm and drought wrecked their crops, disputed inheritances rent them apart, and hideous accidents and premature death afflicted them.

Every fresh misfortune brought me new delight, for I had cursed them all, except for my own son. When I was condemned, I was pregnant, and later the child was taken from me at birth. As soon as he was old enough to understand, he was told his mother was dead, and the woman to whom nobody spoke was a distant relative gone stark mad. For my own part I never approached him, for fear that they would make him share my shame. I suffered for years, watching him grow, unable to reach out to him as a mother. Later, his adolescent grace and fragility made me think of Chrétien.

When his father, my husband, died young, my status changed. I was now the mother of the seigneur, and no longer an adulterous wife. I was still ostracized, but people began to smile at me again, and for the first time the slimy priest offered me more than absolution. He proposed that my son be told who I was. I declined the offer. I did not want my boy to bear the guilt of his father and his father's family, who had done me so great a wrong. I told the priest I needed nothing, and certainly not a convent, nor the kindliness of nuns.

All that mattered to me was to remain near my son; I wanted no change; I wanted to protect him. Every day I prayed for him, willing that handsome, gifted youth to succeed. But he did not.

Instead he lost battle after battle throughout his life, in court, in business, and on the field of conflict. His children died in infancy and he was unhappy in his marriage. Yet he bore up bravely against the misfortunes bred of my hatred—for that was what they were. He acquired the nickname "Luckless," and gradually his fortune declined and his castle fell into ruin.

By the time I fell into my last illness, he was already exhausted by his struggle against adversity. The priest who came to my deathbed again offered to bring my son to my side, but again I declined. I would not inflict this ultimate blow upon him. Then the slimy priest began to speak of forgiveness for those who had brought me to ruin: but I hated them all the more, holding them responsible not only for my own misfortune, but for my son's also. Not so long before, one of their number, a cousin of my husband's, had come to seek amends. He too I had sent away.

"Forgive them," begged the priest.

"I will not," I answered, with my last breath.

THE SECRET DUEL

Schloss Schwarzenraben, Westphalia, Germany

THE FIRST STRANGE THING I noticed was the light.

It was gray-gold, and it seemed to come from nowhere. We were in the broad plain of Westphalia; the landscape of fields bordered with hedges and woodlands was tranquil in the extreme. After driving down a long avenue of lime trees, we entered a first courtyard surrounded by outbuildings, in the French style, leading across a working drawbridge to the main yard of the castle of Schwarzenraben. The latter rose from the still waters of an encircling moat, whose banks were gripped by hundred-year-old trees. The style of the house was Baroque and elegant, dating from the second half of the eighteenth century.

Like all houses of the region, Schwarzenraben is constructed on tremendous pilings sunk into the once-swampy soil of Westphalia. A great local family, the Hördes, were its builders, but nobody knows how the castle received its peculiar sobriquet "Black Crow." It seems there was a much smaller dwelling here before, which an arrogant Hörde pulled down and replaced. This Hörde was a high official in the service of the Prince-Archbishop of Cologne, Clement Augustus of Bavaria. He is said to have invited the sovereign here to hunt, whereupon the latter (a wretched hand with a gun)

shot his leg full of pellets. Thereafter the remorseful Clement Augustus showered his victim with honors and rewards, ultimately enabling Hörde to build a princely residence.

Schwarzenraben was eventually inherited by the Kettelers, an old Westphalian family. In the last century one of the Kettelers, who was Archbishop of Munster, was in the forefront of social progress in Germany. As well as being honest and law-abiding, the Kettelers were staunch patriots and refined art-lovers, as their collection of objects and paintings testifies.

We were greeted by Baroness Maria von Ketteler herself, who, despite her eighty-seven years and the rheumatism which makes her every movement a martyrdom, remains a model of old-fashioned courtesy. She also has a bright eye, a lively interest in everything, inexhaustible gusto, and a gargantuan appetite for life. Leaning on her cane, she insisted on personally showing us around her castle.

We began by climbing a majestic staircase, with a ceilingful of putti writhing overhead. Then we passed through a series of salons beautifully accommodated with marquetry furniture, whose walls were hung with rows of portraits of ancestors. We lingered to admire rococo ballrooms and studies decorated with stuccos as finely wrought as lace. Finally, we halted in a private chapel peopled by gilded, wildly gesticulating saints.

I inquired about ghosts. Our hostess believed in them, without admitting it in so many words. In the course of her long life, she had seen so much that the supernatural held little interest for her anymore. On the other hand, she was greatly inhabited by the memory of the last war, and she recounted the dangers she had faced in the course of it with terrific verve.

First there was harassment by the Nazis, then by the Allies. Her husband disappeared, and she had no news of him for many months. There were bombings, and the incursions of prisoners who escaped from a neighboring camp bent on murder and rapine. Refugees poured into the castle by the hundreds and she had somehow to feed them, even though there was no food at all, anywhere. Finally, in April 1944, an American general arrived to requisition the castle, ordering her out within the hour. She took him to the chapel. The American stood for a while in silence, then revoked his order and allowed the baroness to remain, on condition that he be allowed "to bring his officers to this place of worship."

A week later, a second American general arrived with exactly the same demand. What else could she do, but hope for a second miracle? The baroness showed the officer the way to the chapel, even though he told her he was not a Catholic, but a Jew. And he too left her in possession . . .

Seeing her grappling with these insuperable problems of war's aftermath, one of the occupying GIs couldn't resist telling her she'd be a good deal better off in a "two-room walk-up in Chicago."

As she talked on of the past, the baroness led us through to the central reception hall on the second floor of her palace. The perfect oval proportions and lavish decor, the tall tarnished mirrors between the windows overlooking the park, the marble walls covered in portraits of prince-bishops must have made this room the perfect setting for a ball. With a little effort, one could imagine the notes of a spinet echoing here, and couples dancing round and round. The baroness opened a door of exotic wood, giving on to a disused library.

"This," she said, "is where it happened."

Her name was Maria Anna von Hörde, and she lived at the turn of the eighteenth and nineteenth centuries. She was married, reluctantly, to a man she did not love. And while there wasn't a great deal more information than this to be gleaned about her earthly life, her activities after her death appear to have been meticulously recorded.

Maria Anna's mature career as a ghost began in the mid-nineteenth century, at which time a couple of lady cousins of the mistress of the house, expecting to arrive late at the castle, told her not to wait up for them. This was fine: only the next day, they politely thanked their hostess for sending someone out to meet them.

Nobody had been sent, of course. Under close interrogation, the lady cousins described the person they had seen and the clothes she was wearing. The baroness turned pale, and led them to a portrait entitled *The Bible Lady*, whom they instantly identified.

Later Schloss Schwarzenraben was left empty for thirty-odd years. Nobody in the district came near the place, because of its evil reputation and the tremendous curse said to have been laid upon it by the Blue Lady. In the end it was left to Baroness Maria's mother-and father-in-law to bring the old house back to life and outface the Blue Lady.

But first of all, what about the lady? Why was she called this? Quite simply, because she had flaming red hair, as her portrait clearly shows. Red was the color of the devil, not to be mentioned out loud, for fear of attracting his attention; therefore, since nobody in the natural state has blue hair, and since the devil has a powerful aversion to blue, the most risk-free name for the ghost was the Blue Lady.

It should be made clear that this Blue Lady had never disturbed anybody in any way. She never spoke, never appeared to any member of the Ketteler family, and was only seen by servants or guests. What the ser-

vants and guests saw was a fleeting figure on the staircase, in a gallery, in a salon. The lady just floated by and seemed, rather feebly, to want people to pray for her. As soon as this request was understood one way or another, she retired from the scene. Yet was it possible that this same highly discreet phantom can have rapped twice on the shoulder of an old family friend who happened to be looking at her portrait, throwing him into a frenzy of panic?

Only on one other occasion did the Blue Lady become violent—in 1928. At that time a priest still came to the castle on weekends, staying on Saturday night and saying Mass the following morning. One Saturday this priest undertook to prove that ghosts did not exist—and if they did, he bragged that he would exorcise them in a jiffy. With the help of Hermann, one of the servants, this troublesome priest took down the painting of the Blue Lady and laid it under his bed.

Next morning he was so livid and exhausted that he could scarcely get through the responses.

For years afterwards he refused to say what had happened to him during the night, and would get angry at the very mention of it. Finally, however, he unburdened himself to a friend. At three in the morning, he had awakened to find someone sitting on his chest and vigorously attempting to choke him. He tried to thrust his attacker away,

but his hands grasped at thin air and he could see nothing but the ordinary shadows of night. He was half-throttled when he had the wit to shout out: "I'll put you back in your place!" upon which the pressure on his throat abruptly relaxed. Without waiting another moment, he ran to hang the portrait of the Blue Lady where it had been before.

Another priest, this time a Jesuit, appears to have had a much more cordial relationship with the Blue Lady, with whom he consorted on a daily basis in his room adjoining the chapel. One morning, Baroness Maria's mother-in-law awoke with a terrible toothache, and before summoning the local GP, a wise woman was called in from the neighboring town of Lippstadt. The latter passed her hands very slowly over the skull of the dowager baroness and the pain immediately evaporated. At this point in the proceedings, the doctor made his appearance at the gate. What shame if he should discover the witch in the house! The woman was pushed behind the first door, which happened to be that of the Jesuit's room: and the man of God and the witch found themselves face-to-face. She examined the room, immediately "sensed" the presence of the Blue Lady, and kindly offered to rid it of her presence forever. But the Jesuit begged her to do nothing of the sort, explaining that the Blue Lady was his "sole diversion in life."

Baroness Maria's son, Karl von Ketteler, who is the family historian, is reluctant to identify Maria Anna von Hörde as the Blue Lady, given that certain details of her portrait do not tally with the period in which she was supposed to have lived. Moreover, if Maria Anna really was the phantom haunting Schloss Schwarzenraben, she would neither have died in an odor of sanctity nor would she have been buried in the parish church.

I wanted to know, as usual, if there were any attics in the castle. There were, said the baroness, if I didn't mind getting covered in dust; she then handed me the keys and showed me the way. After climbing a dark wooden stairway, Justin and I found ourselves in front of a small door which was very reluctant to open.

Beyond was an immense attic area, stuffed with possessions, which no one had entered for years. There were chairs under covers, odd sections of paneling, frames, wardrobes. Apart from the steel girders which had replaced the original oak beams, this part of the house looked as if it had seen no change for centuries. I squeezed past the indistinct shapes of swathed objects to the darkest—and most upsetting—corner of the attic. Here I drew the black cover from a neo-Gothic sofa and sat myself down in a cloud of hot dust. Around me in the half-light the sheeted outlines of the furniture took on outlandish shapes.

Before long I had the impression of taking wing, and flying across a landscape of hills and valleys, with villages of another epoch far below me. Another castle loomed in my mind, this time of red brick; perhaps the first seat of the Hörde family. Then came the start of a nonsensical tale, disconnected utterances. I suspected that some agency was trying to lure me off the track, that I was straying . . .

Eventually, I opened my eyes and banished the chaotic images. After that it wasn't long before I sensed her presence. I calculated that she was only a few yards away, slightly to my left. A gray figure, or a figure shrouded in gray.

There was something rather unpleasant about her.

My marriage was arranged, in the usual way. The baron who married me, married a wealthy heiress, who was fortunately far from plain. I had been brought up to accept my lot without complaint. It was only after the ceremony, when I had spent a few weeks in his company, that I realized that my husband was not only a woman-hater, but a cruel man to boot. He got children of my body without ever showing me love, and he must have known all too well that he repelled me and that I despised him. I did not want my children, and they lived on without love. And year after year our lives continued entwined—until the war, or rather the wars.

We watched the progress of the French Revolution with apprehension, but also with a certain detachment. It seemed very far away, and

so unreal. Then suddenly it burst upon us, and war came to our very gates. Every time an army marched by, the whole village took refuge at Schwarzenraben. I had to shelter, feed, and console, and prevent theft and looting. I wonder still that we managed to keep our houses and lands, and even our heads, living through those times. The invaders moved to and fro, sowing destruction and misery wherever they went. Occasionally an individual act of generosity or heroism flared up above the general crassness of the wars, but as a rule we lived in an atmosphere of egotism, cowardice, and pettiness. You may think that the presence of such danger colored my existence, and that fear chased away my boredom. It wasn't so: I was strangely indifferent to the great events swirling around us and besieging us. I lived in an atmosphere of menace, but with the sense that I was in the calm eye of the cyclone. One thing is sure, the war did nothing to alleviate my personal unhappiness.

Coquetry became my best remedy for ennui. The provincial aristocrats and the noble ladies of Munster followed the shifts of fashion with passionate interest. The length of a dress, the height of a corsage, and the color of a veil were as important to us as battles, alliances, and treaties. Far worse than the interminable cannonading of our castle was the thought that the latest models from Paris might not reach us in time. Sometimes, after spending hours at my dressing table or in front of my glass, I asked myself for whom I was wearing this daring décolleté, for whom I had draped my shoulders with this scarlet shawl, the tint of

which so admirably set off my flaming chestnut hair. I devoured all the latest novels, and in spite of the drumrolls and the bugle calls that filled the period, I dreamed of romanticism with its wild and melancholy passions.

Before long, love affairs had replaced fashion as my focus of interest. The more I read, the more I identified with the heroines in my books.

One day, a Frenchman was billeted with us. He was an officer in a gold-braided red uniform, an elegant talker with dashing mustaches and black eyes. At a stroke, my coquetry acquired a purpose because I was before his eyes, and my reading became useful because it told me how to behave in his presence. A single compliment slightly more audacious than usual, a single longer look into my eyes, and I was ready to fall straight into his arms.

I was attractive, though not conventionally pretty. I had that air about me which the French call "du chien." My lover told me I was "fiery" and he himself seemed to sparkle like lit gunpowder when he was with me. Yet there was really nothing special about him, he was probably just as pleasing to the farm girls and old maids he consorted with as he was to me. My moral state placed me on a level with these, however. I loved in order not to die, for my husband's coldness and illtreatment had annihilated me to the point where I could scarcely breathe. My liaison gave me oxygen at last. At first I thought myself madly in love with the Frenchman, but soon enough I realized that the only thing binding us was pleasure, the pleasure we so often had of each other in the attic.

He, on the other hand, fell sincerely in love with me.

My husband quite naturally loathed the French Revolution and Bonaparte, which to him were one and the same thing. All he could see was that the old order had been smashed, and the resultant wars had made it impossible to live out his blinkered life on his estates. He could not abide the presence of the cursed French—neither their émigré nobles, nor the Bonapartist soldiers who followed. His rage against them simmered on for years, and was finally focused on the officer he was compelled to lodge. The baron was a heavy man, the Frenchman a light one. The baron was taciturn, the Frenchman as garrulous as a jay. The baron had no success with women at all. The Frenchman's path was littered with broken hearts.

So when the Frenchman began to pay court to me, my husband, seeing I was not unreceptive to his advances, felt a rage that broke all bounds; and it was all the worse because it had no issue. He could be cold and cruel to a passive woman, but he had no answer to one who openly defied him. In the end, however, he found a retort which was worthy of his unspeakable viciousness: his nightly embraces increased tenfold, to my disgust and horror, and I became pregnant.

For many weeks the baron waited patiently for his opportunity. He was hesitant, because he knew there would be a shattering scandal if he were found out. He determined to act as discreetly as possible, and despite his impatience the right moment refused to come. Until that night. . .

For some time he had been in the habit of inviting the Frenchman for an after-dinner game of cards. The first time he did this, his guest (who knew quite well what the baron thought of him) was astonished, but dared not refuse. Then he had to get used to it. On the evening in question the two men sat with me in the corner chamber, which has such delicate stuccos, where we took coffee. The game began, and went on and on. I yawned discreetly in my armchair. My husband watched me covertly, as if he were waiting only for me to retire.

At last the game ended. The Frenchman made to rise, but the baron requested another hand and he sat down again reluctantly. I decided to retire to bed.

After my departure, the baron refused to deal; he merely waited. He had drawn out the first game in order to make sure the whole household would be fast asleep and hear nothing. Now he was waiting for me to go to sleep. The Frenchman watched, intrigued. The baron avoided his glance, holding the pack of cards so tightly in his hand that he crumpled it.

Finally he spoke. He was always a man of few words and now without more ado he challenged his rival to a duel — to the death. "I'm sure you know exactly why," he added. The Frenchman immediately took up the challenge, and the baron then suggested they go to one of the upper floors, as far away as possible from the rest of the household.

The room chosen was lit by a few torches, and moonlight flooded in through the tall bay windows. The two men drew their swords.

In the fight that ensued, the heavier baron had an advantage in the sheer fury of his onslaught. The Frenchman was a far better swordsman, but he was fatigued by the afternoon he had spent in my arms, and above all by the interminable evening. His first sally narrowly missed the baron, who responded with a furious headlong lunge, bursting through the Frenchman's defense and sending the blade through his body, skewering him so violently through the heart that the steel guard crashed against his ribs. The Frenchman fell dead on the carpet, and my husband, having withdrawn his sword from the corpse, walked to the window and flung it into the moat. Then he turned on his heel and left the room.

I think that one reason why the baron prepared his stroke so carefully was that he too, without knowing it, was curiously attracted to the French officer. Nevertheless, by challenging, fighting, and killing his wife's lover, my husband did not act solely out of jealousy; he may also have sought to destroy a thing which was inaccessible to him, to smash a sentiment which to him was entirely odious. The Frenchman had accepted the duel on condition that I would never know it had taken place, and my husband held to this — at first.

When the baron had killed his rival, he slipped into my bedroom where I lay pretending to be asleep. I felt him come near and stare at me for a long moment. Then he quietly withdrew. In the small hours of the morning, he had his rival's body spirited away. This was done by the servants, who cordially loathed the French for the suffering and hardship they had brought upon us and were only too happy to do this service for their master.

Next day my husband told me that the Frenchman had received urgent orders in the night, and had left directly. There was nothing particularly surprising about this, and I saw no reason to doubt it. I missed my lover, but in general his absence caused me only minor grief.

Before day my husband told me that the Frenchman had received urgent orders in the night, and had left directly. There was nothing particularly surprising about this, and I saw no reason to doubt it. I missed my lover, but in general his absence caused me only minor grief.

Before long I was immersed in preparations for the birth of my baby. It was a boy, and as soon as I saw him I was gripped by an insistent doubt. He could have been sired by either man. I stared at his eyes, his hair, and his mouth; I would have stared into his soul had it been possible. My uncertainty tore me apart, for according as I imputed him to the baron or to the Frenchman, my feelings toward him changed.

Despite this doubt, which made him attractive and repulsive to me by turns, the child's very existence served as a useful barrier between my husband and myself. I wondered if the baron had the same doubts as I did. Anyway, he carefully avoided the boy, who had only to enter a room for my husband to rush out, as if the child's presence was some kind of dire threat to him.

Then one day, when my son was about four, he took him away without telling me where they were going. They were absent for a week, at the end of which I heard a traveling carriage roll into the courtyard. I saw my husband and son get out together, and climb the stairs to my boudoir. The boy was parchment white. My husband thrust him forward roughly.

"Your lover is dead, I killed him. And now here is your bastard, who has been castrated, so there will be no issue."

Those words turned me to stone, and for the rest of our lives together in this house of misery, I was stone.

My husband's vengeance brought him no satisfaction whatever, for he too lapsed into impenetrable morbidity. In my despair, I was unable even to show my son the pity I felt for him, and though he grew physically, his mind never evolved from its state of prostration. Little by little, the life

drained out of him; he died, and very soon I too was dead, though I was still young.

Is life really worth our love of it, with all its cheats and disappointments? My existence was comprehensively wrecked, through no fault of my own, and there are others like me beyond counting. Circumstances alone have the power to build or destroy human beings. Even death has been unjust to me, for my ghost is taken to be that of the Blue Lady, a noble and pious ancestress who was buried in the choir of the chapel.

And I am alone. This waiting is hard for me. When I arrived at the supreme moment of passing, I fell back, a prisoner of my own misfortune. I am a ghost because I never learned to love. If only I had been unhappy in love, instead of unhappy because I could not love.

THE WITCHES' WELL

Gleichenberg, Styria, Austria

COUNT TRAUTTMANSDORFF WAS desperately worried. He belonged to a venerable and illustrious family, he was lord of a cluster of castles which made him the virtual master of all Styria, and in his hands were concentrated most of the highest offices in the court of the Emperor Ferdinand. Yet he had one insuperable problem, the problem of his issue. He had no heir but a sickly boy with weak lungs, who gave every indication of dying young. And if he did die young, the Trauttmansdorff line would be extinguished with him, to the inconsolable grief of his father. As far as the count could see, only a miracle could avert this outcome.

One day, the child was taking the woodland air with his nurse, close by the count's fortress of Gleichenberg, in the vain hope that some improvement might result. Suddenly a Gypsy woman emerged from the trees: the governess made to run away, but the Gypsy retained her, saying she meant no harm.

"Listen: I have watched the two of you for months now, you and this puny boy. If you do nothing, he will certainly die. Do as I say: go to the bottom of the valley, and there under a great rock you will find a spring. Let this child drink from it."

With that, the Gypsy woman left them.

The nurse said nothing of this encounter

to anyone, but later, having nothing to lose, she went down to the bottom of the valley, found the spring (hidden though it was in the undergrowth), and brought back a cup of water which she gave to her charge. After a few weeks, the boy took a turn for the better, and the nurse found the courage to tell Count Trauttmansdorff what she had done. The count himself remembered that he had heard of the Romans prizing the thermal waters thereabouts for their usefulness in the treatment of pulmonary ailments. Since their time, the springs had been entirely forgotten.

Now Count Trauttmansdorff gave orders that the Gypsy woman be sought out and brought before him, and when she was, he took the heavy gold chain from around his neck and placed it upon hers. Thereafter his son and heir grew apace in strength and courage. The story of the cure spread far and wide, and other sick people came to drink at the spring and were healed. The reputation of the spring grew and grew and even today—thanks to the Gypsy woman—Gleichenberg is famed throughout Austria for its waters.

When Count Trauttmansdorff died, the son he had expected to lose in infancy inherited all his fortune and his titles, becoming one of Emperor Ferdinand's most trusted counselors and a famous and successful leader of his armies. And at Gleichenberg he continued the family tradition of administering justice.

One day, an old crone dressed in filthy rags was dragged before him, in the final stages of decay and indigence. She had committed some small larceny. The count was preparing to pass sentence when the woman raised her head and croaked: "I saved your life long ago. Now save mine!" As she spoke, she produced the gold chain of the count's father from under her rags. So the count pardoned the Gypsy woman and saw that she wanted for nothing for the rest of her days.

Many years later, the same Count Trauttmansdorff was sitting in judgment in a case of witchcraft, in the great hall of his fortress. We may imagine the scene: the Renaissance chairs, the rough medieval masonry, the rich tapestries and hangings suspended from rings set in the walls, the narrow windows, the torchlight glimmering on dark wood. One corner of the room was occupied by a kind of stone tower, with a small opening and a dome. Gleichenberg then was less of a private dwelling than the residence of the emperor's representative, and its disposition reflected the coldness of the administrative power.

Before the gilded throne occupied by Count Trauttmansdorff stood a group of peasant women, shackled to each other. They numbered about a score, and they were all dressed in gaudy tatters and cheap jewelry. Their matted hair was studded with artificial flowers and feathers, and they were protesting loudly, threatening to call down havoc on the heads of their tormentors. Their curses were horrible to hear.

Count Trauttmansdorff had read the charges against them in detail. In the great hall of the castle at Gleichenberg, everybody, from the subtlest freethinking lawyers to the most grizzled veterans of the wars against the Turks, was terrified. All were ready to believe that these women could summon the devil himself into their midst. Only the count himself was unaffected; he saw the frightened looks passing between the women, even as they spat their threats and insults. He also saw the hate-filled faces and the naked weapons of the guards glittering in the torchlight. He remembered that it was a Gypsy woman, one like some of these, who had saved his life and the lives of many others. He was far from convinced that they would harm a fly.

Yet the church, the emperor, and the law demanded savage retribution against all such suspected daughters of the Evil One. And as he listened to their detailed descriptions of their practices, he began in spite of himself to feel a creeping dread of the unknown. Around him, the tension had reached breaking point. All those present wished to rid themselves of the menace the witches represented, to wake from the nightmare they had induced.

The count made his decision. They must be annihilated, as swiftly as possible. He made a sign to the guards . . .

"This castle has always been rather sad and gloomy," says its present owner, Countess Annie Stubenberg, a tall, strong, straight-backed person of about seventy who has the energy of a much younger woman. She is a worthy representative of the robust Trauttmansdorff line, from which she is descended on her mother's side. Their history, which can be followed in detail from the fourteenth century onward, is intricately linked to that of the Hapsburgs, and generation after generation, they occupied the highest offices in the empire. In this way they earned much honor, but at the same time there was a constant strain of misfortune in their affairs, which Countess Annie attributes to the curse left on the family by the witches.

In effect, ever since the famous witchcraft trial, the history of Gleichenberg has been a tragic litany. The first—and perhaps the worst—horror was that of the Countess Trauttmansdorff, who during the war with the Turks witnessed the arrival at the castle of twenty-one corpses, the entire complement of her sons and nephews. For century upon century after, ghosts proliferated in the castle with the clear intention (or so it seemed) of driving out its living inmates. But these inmates somehow remained stolidly indifferent to everything the ghosts could do. Countess Annie remembers her grandfather, for example, in whose bedroom there was such a continual din of slamming doors, crashing windows, and lids of chests opening and shutting that when the poor man repaired to his palace in Vienna, the silence made him so jumpy he couldn't sleep a wink.

One day a Hungarian princess arrived to stay, who was eccentric enough to deny the existence of ghosts. Not one of the hair-raising stories she was told could shake her conviction, and when in the night she was awakened by a deafening racket in the passage outside her room, she thought the children were pulling her leg. Furious, she strode to the door—there was nobody outside—and marched straight to the bedroom of Count Trauttmansdorff himself, where she demanded that the culprits be punished. The count (Annie's father) calmed her down and escorted her back to her room, which was found to be locked on the inside. A locksmith had to be called out in the middle of the night, before the chastened princess

could resume her slumbers, much troubled by dreams of witchcraft.

The father of Countess Annie finally decided to rid himself of the witches once and for all, but without arousing the suspicions of the villagers, who were thoroughly superstitious. With this in mind, he brought several workers from a distant city, who on his instructions excavated a whole pile of debris before coming upon a score or so of skeletons. A cursory examination showed that all of these bones were female, and many bore easily recognizable traces of wounds inflicted by swords. On the orders of the count, the workmen buried all the skeletons in a far corner of the forest, and covered them over with a layer of cement followed by another layer of soil. They operated at night so that nobody could see what they were doing, and in order that the exact burial site should remain a secret; after which, having sworn to say nothing, they dispersed.

The ensuing interlude of peace did not last very long. The count's wife was sitting on the steps reading, when she heard the dinner bell sound and looked up to see an old woman, grotesquely dressed in a green bolero and red skirt, drifting by on the terrace. "Who are you? What are you doing here?" she called out, but the woman continued to the battlements, swung a leg over the parapet, and vanished. The countess rushed in pursuit, sure that she would see a crumpled corpse at the foot of the rampart: but there was no one, alive or dead, to be seen.

Several months later, while she was visiting a local church, the same countess was brought up short by a painting of a very old, very ugly woman wearing the same clothes as she had seen on the rampart. The picture was entitled *Witch of Gleichenberg*.

The ghosts finally prevailed in their crusade to scare the living out of Gleichenberg in the course of the last war. As it had been in the Middle Ages, Gleichenberg remained a strategic fortress in the twentieth century, and a fierce battle was fought over it. It changed hands six times between the S.S. and the Red Army, and when its owners finally reclaimed its shattered ruins at the end of the war, complete abandonment looked like the wisest solution. The roofs were completely destroyed, and everything within had been wrecked or looted. But Countess Annie and her husband, both of them fiercely attached to their property, refused to be daunted. They moved into an outbuilding and immediately set about the first vital repairs, at about the time when the first refugees were beginning to trickle in from the East, hotly pursued by the Soviets.

By the time Count Hunyadi, an old friend from before the war, arrived at their door, there was no room left for him in the outbuildings, and Countess Annie offered him all she had—a room in the bombed-out castle. She warned him that he would have to take his chances alone against the swarms of phantoms.

Next morning Count Hunyadi arrived at breakfast looking calm and refreshed. He had heard a number of invisible visitors tramping through his room, along with packs of hounds baying in the courtyard and horses whinnying in the stables. But, as he said, he had seen so many outrages committed by the living that nothing the dead could manage would ever scare him again.

The next night, Countess Annie had her guest's bedroom door nailed shut. Crossed halberds were placed across the door frame, and the heaviest Renaissance chest in the house was shoved against it. But the next morning, before Count Hunyadi even woke, she was able to see with her own eyes that the door had been smashed down and both halberds and chest had been displaced to the center of the gallery.

Nevertheless, she persevered with the restoration of the castle and eventually moved into it again. The ghosts, who were no doubt enraged by this, struck back: on three occasions over a very few years, the castle burned down. The final fire took place at night, and for miles around people saw the flames leaping upward from the hilltop. After this, the owners finally admitted defeat. They moved back into the charming outbuildings and abandoned the castle proper to its brambles, its jackdaws, and its ghosts. Nature gradually crept in, surrounding Schloss Gleichenberg with impenetrable vegetation like Sleeping Beauty's palace.

Justin and I arrived by car one winter morning, after driving through the steep valleys and forests of Styria, on whose peaks stood stronghold after stronghold. The watering place of Gleichenberg, which is filled to bursting in the summer season, was completely quiet. The big hotels were closed and the streets were empty of people.

Countess Annie received us in her charming house with the warmth, simplicity, and grace which are so characteristic of central Europe. From the windows we could see the ruins of her ancestral home, whose shattered walls pointed at the sky like black fingers.

Since the final fire, Annie had only set foot in the castle once. A prince of Europe's greatest royal house, well versed in the occult, happened to pay her a visit and suggested that they should summon the witches in the basement beneath the great hall,

where their skeletons had been excavated. Those present had not been disappointed: lightning flashed from the floor, a knight in armor had seized the spiritualist prince by the shoulders and lifted him off the ground, and a huge yellow dog with horns, a well-known manifestation of the arch-fiend, had showed himself very clearly. Countess Annie is still perfectly certain that her old castle possessed every iota of its malign power; and from time to time visitors who dare to venture into its ruins confirm the fact.

"People often come knocking at my door to complain that unseen children have been slinging stones at them up there."

There are no children at Schloss Gleichenberg.

Although she claims that she wants nothing more to do with the terrible old place, Annie is still curious about the secrets she so dreads. A venerable rumor has it that miles of secret passages converge on the building from different directions. Only recently, masons shoring up a wall saw a giant hole open up before them, which Countess Annie hurriedly made them block up again, for fear they might release some other long-buried witch.

Many years before, against her better judgment, she allowed her cousins to search among the castle's foundations. They bur-

rowed through the bushes and entered using ladders and miner's lamps, lowering themselves down wellshafts on long ropes. They discovered, among other things, huge underground rooms; but at this point Annie called a halt to their investigations. "I didn't want them to come to any harm," she explains simply.

Then it came to her ears that certain people knew their way around these underground halls and were using them to conduct mysterious nocturnal assemblies. She followed up this information, which eventually led her to a local antique dealer.

Wearing a wig and glasses, she entered the man's shop and found nobody at home, whereupon she explored it at her leisure. A wooden ladder led up to an office which she couldn't resist examining, and here she found paintings and furniture which she suspected had been stolen from other castles in the vicinity. She was in the storehouse of a receiver of stolen goods. At this juncture the man himself appeared, looking threatening. He was in the process of throwing her out by main force when she saw a flicker of recognition cross his face.

"Countess, instead of poking around my shop, why don't you go through the archives of the Landesmuseum at Gratz?"

With this, he slammed the door in her face.

Annie immediately followed this advice and was stunned to discover a fat file marked "Plans of the underground area of Schloss Gleichenberg." She opened it, only to discover the detailed plans of a modern villa. The original contents had been stolen. By whom? Why?

The countess took all these inexplicable facts as so many warnings, and her earnest advice to us was not to go near the invisible inhabitants of the fortress of Gleichenberg, now that they were at last the masters of the place.

"They're violent and aggressive," she assured me. "Don't go there—I'm frightened for you."

But her affectionate attempts to warn me off only increased my impatience. Fortified by her recommendations—and I think her prayers—we took our leave.

Along the path, the thorns and brambles grew thicker and more troublesome the farther we progressed. The bridge was almost entirely collapsed, and the snow and mud made the narrow passage slippery and perilous. More than once we nearly fell into the moat. On the far side, we came up against a giant iron gate, at least three hundred years old, which creaked wearily open when we pushed. After this we scrambled up a muddy slope, grasping at roots for balance and nearly falling into deep trenches covered over with ivy. By way of a second partly collapsed gateway, we entered the main courtyard, and here a surprise awaited us, for in the middle of the rubble and shrubs a single facade remained intact, with its graceful arcades and loggias. This place was sweetly reminiscent of Italy, despite the desolation all around.

The castle was otherwise totally devastated by fire and the action of time and weather. There was silence, inertia, and lurking somewhere nearby an indefinable menace. The light began to fade, though the February sun still shone brightly. I climbed to the highest point I could reach, the lip of a wall overhanging a precipice. All around me the countryside stretched away for mile upon mile, its meadows and woodlands merging together in the long gray-blue winter shadows. On the horizon, the dark clouds were tinged with crimson. The tranquillity of evening enveloped me, and curiously I thought it not incompatible with the possible presence of witches. Then I picked my way down through the snow-covered rubble until at last I found myself in the great hall, where long ago the witches had been judged and condemned. Like twisted arms, the roots of shrubs had begun to break through the walls. The high wall at the back of the room still held, towering behind the smashed open ceilings. Fifteen feet in thickness, this

wall had once held out for several months under the incessant cannonades of King Ottokar of Bohemia.

In the most distant corner, despite the shadows invading the room, I could make out the silhouette of a little round turret, topped by a dome. This must be the famous witches' well.

I walked up and down and across this desolate space, oppressed by a sense of utter solitude. I was far from everything and everyone else alive. The witches were by me. But I knew now that I had nothing to fear from them. On the contrary, there was someone else present who alarmed me not a little. A soft noise made me jump: probably a pebble coming off the wall. I went on with my pacing, compelling myself to drive off the anxiety which was insinuating itself into my being. I wasn't wanted here at all, I could feel, but whatever it was that was rejecting me, *it was not the witches.*

Then I let out a cry. A great stone had fallen just beside me, passing close enough to touch my coat . . . I stood paralyzed, my heart beating like a jackhammer, until I sensed the danger slowly heaving itself away.

We are ghosts, but we are less wretched by far than those who condemned us to death. We dance and laugh: we're not sinister or threatening at all. Nor were we sinister in life. We dabbled a

little in black magic, we invoked spirits, but these days all that would be thought mere child's play. We belonged to well-off farming families in the district, but in general we were ignorant girls, ignorant of the gravity of what we got up to at our witches' sabbaths. We thought ourselves powerful sorceresses capable of changing the world, but we were novices. We were bored and our boredom led us to this. Our husbands spent their time in the fields, and although we had children and houses to occupy us, we had help for these and they didn't satisfy us. Above all, we were carried away by the atmosphere of the time—which was one of the war, invasion, and religious conflict. Europe was awash with blood; traditional beliefs and old values had lost their sense. All was confusion, flux, and turbulence. And we were carried away like everybody else, as our ancestral faith crumbled around us.

Then we came into contact with a real witch. She understood the possibilities offered by our state of mind and our availability. She corrupted us and initiated us, leading us into the world of darkness without giving us the true key to it, having us believe that we had sufficient power and knowledge to navigate safely through it.

Guided by the witch, we concocted love philters for one another (we never ventured on poisons at any time). We cast spells, with no result. But we saw how the spells of our chief witch were invariably successful, and devastatingly so.

We gathered for our sabbaths in an isolated part of the country, and there we invoked the Evil One. The ease with which he could be made to appear strengthened our illusion of power. He came to us as a yellow dog, as a billy goat, or as some other monstrous animal. The devil, whose name blankets very dark powers which live so near to us, is ready to show himself at the slightest request.

Suddenly, our initiator abandoned us utterly. She had had wind that we were threatened. She vanished like the mist: but we, who remained under her spell, could not perceive the peril that was approaching us. We threw away all caution, and in the euphoria of our wretched little successes, we sought to enlarge our circle by inviting other women to join us. One of these told all to the authorities, and we were apprehended and brought to the castle in chains.

Our trial took place in this great hall, and it lasted for many days. In their naïveté and eagerness to prove their own innocence, the women we had sought to initiate exaggerated their charges, painting us as we would have loved to be, as the most powerful of witches. Only one witness told the truth, the husband of one of our number who had heard all about us from his woman—and had laughed. When she described to him our spells and our attempts to raise the Evil One, he laughed even louder: but now, knowing we were in real danger, he tried to save us. He told the count exactly what he had told his wife, that these so-called sabbaths were women's nonsense, so much foolishness.

This man's view found an echo in the governor

of the province, Count Trauttmansdorff, who headed the tribunal. This sensible man had no desire whatever to send us to our deaths. His opinion was that we should be publicly whipped as a punishment for our foolishness. The count therefore did what he could to lend weight to the husband's testimony.

But there were other accusers involved, notably the failed priest and advocate who stood behind the count's throne. This low creature was eaten up with envy and ambition; he longed for fame and power, but nobody paid any attention to him. For years he had awaited his hour; now our trial offered him the opportunity he craved. With diabolical cunning and mastery of legal niceties, this manipulator demolished the testimony of the husband and frightened Count Trauttmansdorff into believing that leniency in this case would sow disorder throughout the province, with dire consequences for his own overlordship.

At first, with his soft speeches, he seemed to be a kindly friend to us, not a ruthless adversary. Pretending to seek attenuating circumstances, he drew us into saying things that worsened our plight still further. Finally, he won over all the witnesses, the judges, and even ourselves, and achieved a sentence of death. We were condemned to be hurled alive into the wellshaft—there, in the corner of the hall.

Our executioners were much more frightened of us than we of them. That advocate had created such a psychosis of terror that nobody cared to lay their hands upon us. Despite their urgings, we not unnaturally refused to leap to our deaths. So they pushed us forward, stabbing at us with their swords and halberds. Some of us were run through and killed; others were sorely wounded and flung themselves in despair into the black hole before them. Those who continued to resist were ruthlessly mutilated before joining their sisters at the bottom of the witches' well—which was never a well at all, of course. Even in their haste to finish their horrible jobs, the executioners would never have been mad enough to hurl us into a cistern, where our rotting bodies would have polluted the castle's drinking water for months. In those times of constant warfare, there was often no time and no room to bury the dead, wherefore they would be left in a deep, dry, well-ventilated shaft, where they could decompose rapidly without poisoning the air of the fortress.

Our trial was a great boon for the man who won our execution. At first his career was meteoric, but later, puffed up with pride, he overstepped the mark and dared to defy the great ones he had formerly obeyed. For this he was once again hurled back into obscurity, and so died.

Count Trauttmansdorff never forgot the cruel execution he had ordered. He became convinced that he had perpetrated a great injustice, for which he incessantly implored God's forgiveness, until he too went down to the grave.

But seen from this side, our tragic end served an occult purpose. We were punished for having

gained access to secrets that were none of our affair, and for having dealt lightly with dark knowledge. There are forces, both positive and negative, which may only be handled by initiates. Those who use them for misdirected purposes, those who broadcast their secrets, those who do not possess sufficient energy, understanding, and purity to dominate the forces they awaken become the victims of such forces. We were just such victims.

Now we stand in need of prayer. Any prayer, to any deity in any place of worship, will help us, and the millions like us, toward the light.

Countless are the beings who die tragically and remain in the world as ghosts—for a time. Only a very few show themselves. Why we should be able to do this, we cannot know; yet those of us who appear do so to draw attention to some fact, or else to give warning. We of Gleichenberg are here to drive away visitors, and for this purpose we inspire terror in a way we never did when we were alive.

This castle, because of the legends surrounding it, attracts people who are mostly harmless: ghost-hunters like yourself, and would-be sorcerers who come to look for shreds of power and petty secrets. They are close to what we used to be, they do much as we did; they have the will to power, but not the

power itself. They make sport of what they do, all unaware in this place of the gigantic peril which hovers silently around, above and beneath them.

In this place immeasurable energies lie buried. Used wisely, they can bestow youth and strength, like the water in the spring; which explains why, despite the massacres and dramas that have taken place at Gleichenberg, the site is still overwhelmingly benign. Many men have come here in the course of history, bringing with them their ambitions, their forces, and their cruelties. Wherefore the buried energy has responded with eruptions of violence and bloodletting. Every stone of this fortress has been drenched in blood. Three times it has burned. Now it is abandoned, and the dark powers inhabiting it are slowly starving for want of human nourishment. One day they will vanish altogether; but until that time comes the danger will be real and present.

Our mission is to stand guard, but we are far from alone. Other tragedies than ours have taken place within these walls, the memory of which must never be stirred. There are many black things here, unquiet things capable of inflicting great harm.

You should block your ears now, and go away, and never come back.

You living people, you understand so little about us.

Of course you mourn your dead but only because you miss them. We need your thoughts and your prayers. We need the energy you do not realize you possess . . . to help us, to better our condition of unhappy waiting.

As you stray through the world's shadows, spare a thought now and then for those on the other side. Every time you think of us or pray for us, a firework will burst into the heavens, and the light it creates will shower down upon you, will help you and will enlighten you.

ACKNOWLEDGMENTS

We wish to extend our special thanks to those who helped in the compilation of the various chapters of this book, as well as to those whose stories could not be included for lack of space. Here are their names, in the chronological order of our researches and travels: Prince di Soragna, Contessa Violante Visconti, Princesse Alexandra de Chimay, John Nicolas Colclough, John and Fiona Bellingham, Mrs. Elizabeth Hickeys, Arthur Montgomery, Mme. Bruno Van der Broek, the Duchesse de Brissac, Mlle. Adélaïde de Clermont-Tonnerre, M. le Marquis and Mme. la Marquise de Beaumont, Count Johannes Nostitz, Comtesse Annie Stubenberg, Comtesse Andrea Stubenberg, Comtesse Maïdi Goess, Lucas Praun, Philippe Manet, Viscountess Rose de Porto da Cruz, Countess Maria Luisa de Villa Flore, Countess Marie José de Villena, M. and Mme. Philippe Nothomb, the Duke and Duchess de Segorbe, Doña Luisa Moxo, Mme. la Marquise de San Mori, the Duke of La Palata, Doña Feli Odriofola, Count Christophe Meran, Baron Karl von Ketteler, Baron and Baroness Clemens von Ketteler, Andres Marshall, Mrs. Gaby Mikelis, Lord Courtenay, Michael Thomasson, Mme. Paul Annick Weiller, Igor Mitoraj, Barbara Koenig, Jacek Kiec, Witt Karol Wojtowicz, Sergiusz Michalcruk, His Royal Highness the Prince Consort of Denmark, Count Ahlefeld-Laurvig, Einer Lange, Erik Iuel, Louba Bogdanova, Andreï Maylunas, Ludmila Koval, Nathalie Lavriovna, M. and Mme. Alexandre Lagoya, Mme. Catherine Le Couey.

We would also like to extend our special thanks to the Baroness Maria von Ketteler, who to our sorrow died a few weeks after so warmly receiving us at Schloss Schwarzenraben.

We would also like to thank those involved in the creation of this book: Yannis

Petsopoulos, Misha Anikst, Edouard Sottocosa for his patience, Akira Nashi for the quality of his prints, Dominique Toutain, Rene Bonnefois, and Jo Anne Metsch for the design.

—Michael of Greece and
Justin Creedy Smith

Hertzog, Patrick de Bourgues, Georges Antaki, and Jeremy Seal.

Above all, I wish to thank the Guardian Angel and Michel, without whom there would have been no light.

—Justin Creedy Smith

I wish to take this opportunity to thank my family and my friends, particularly for their advice and help with the photography: Simon Kitching, Patricia Grenier and the Studio d'Alésia, Jacques Denarnaud, Nicoletta Santoro, Peter Lindbergh, Vincent Dixon, Joel Laiter, and Ian Thomas who still watches over me.

On this road to Damascus, I would like to thank Nori Yasui, Kasumiko Murakami, Hitoshi Okamoto, Kumiko Oga, Gilles

My warmest gratitude goes to Dominique Patry for her dedicated research, to Mme. Odile de Crépy for her speed and application in typing the manuscript, and to Olivier, Patrick, and Mme. Thérése-Marie Mahé for their astute and invaluable critical advice. Most of all, I wish to thank Marina, who had the patience to read five successive versions of this book, and the stamina to keep suggesting improvements right through to the end.

—Michael of Greece